"*47* is upbeat, inspiring, deceptively complex and, on occasion, hysterically funny. . . . Let yourself fly away to a world that now exists only in the memories of historians, and the imagination of artists such as Walter Mosley."

— Steven Barnes, Emmy Award winner and author of *Lion's Blood*, on *All Things Considered*, NPR and NPR.com

"A stirring story of escape from slavery in which [science fiction] and African American myth blend with the realism of plantation brutality and the courage of resistance."
— *Booklist*

"Combing African-American folklore, history, and science fiction, Mosley creates an original tale that speaks to multiple audiences on multiple levels, one that lands squarely and soundly in the gap caused by the paucity of black fantasy and science fiction for young adults."
— *The Bulletin of the Center for Children's Books*

"Time travel, shape-shifting, and intergalactic conflict add unusual, provocative elements to this story. And yet, well-drawn characters; lively dialogue filled with gritty regional dialect; vivid descriptions; and poignant reflections ground it in harsh reality."
— *School Library Journal*

"Thrilling on many levels, the book's voices, sacrifices, climactic battles, and satisfying escapes will dazzle and provoke readers."
— *Horn Book*

"In this haunting, tightly written tale, Mosley insists it is indeed possible to transcend the chains of domination and submission."
— *Seattle Times*

"Deftly written, the story thoroughly involves the reader in a world that resembles our own, but which is also very different."
— *Science Fiction Chronicle*

"A wonderful, genre-bending exploration into life, destiny and what it means to be free."
— *BookPage*

"The story of High John the Conqueror was well known within the American slave population before the Civil War. Walter Mosley takes a fresh and fascinating look at the legend and his magical powers."
— Walter Dean Myers, author of *Monster*

"*47* is magical, engrossing, meaningful, and entertaining. Walter Mosley has written a story for all ages and all races, for readers of fantasy, as well as those who prefer mainstream—in short, a story for all human beings. That's quite an accomplishment."
— Kevin J. Anderson, author of the Saga of Seven Suns series

"This is a heartfelt, spiritual and hopeful book. With the publication of *47*, Walter Mosley confirms his place as one of the world's most important contemporary novelists; he is, indeed, a pure writer of unlimited intelligence and talent."
— Haki R. Madhubuti, poet, author, and distinguished university professor and director of the MFA program in Creative Writing at Chicago State University

"*47* is powerful, evoking the pains of slavery, yet it is uplifting in its use of the fantastic, timeless message. Mosley has done it again with his artful magic and gritty truth."
— Gregory Benford, author of *The Sunborn*

by Walter Mosley

LITTLE, BROWN AND COMPANY
New York • Boston

Little, Brown and Company

Hachette Book Group
237 Park Avenue, New York, NY 10017
Visit our website at www.lb-teens.com

Little, Brown and Company is a division of Hachette Book Group, Inc.
The Little, Brown name and logo are trademarks of Hachette Book Group, Inc.

First Paperback Edition: November 2006
First published in hardcover in May 2005 by Little, Brown and Company

The characters and events portrayed in this book are fictitious. Any similarity to real persons, living or dead, is coincidental and not intended by the author.

Library of Congress Cataloging-in-Publication Data

Mosley, Walter.
  47 / Walter Mosley.—1st ed.
    p. cm.
    Summary: Number 47, a fourteen-year-old slave boy growing up under the watchful eye of a brutal master in 1832, meets the mysterious Tall John, who introduces him to a magical science and also teaches him the meaning of freedom.
    HB ISBN 0-316-11035-3   PB ISBN-10 0-316-01635-7   ISBN-13 978-0-316-01635-3
    [1. Slavery—Fiction. 2. African Americans—Fiction. 3. Plantation life—Fiction.
4. Freedom—Fiction. 5. Magic—Fiction. 6. Georgia—History—1775-1865—Fiction.]
I. Title: Forty-seven. II. Title.

PZ7.M8498Aae 2005
[Fic]—dc22   2004012500

PB 10 9 8 7 6 5 4 3

RRD-IN

Printed in the United States of America

For Sally McCartin
—W.M.

preface

The story you are about to read concerns certain events that occurred in the early days of my life. It all happened over a hundred and seventy years ago. For many of you it might sound like a tall tale because I am no older today than I was back there in the year 1832. But this is no whopper I'm telling; it is a story about my boyhood as a slave and my fated encounter with the amazing Tall John from beyond Africa, who could read dreams, fly between galaxies, and make friends with any animal no matter how wild.

There are many things in the world that most people don't know about. For instance, when I was young nobody ever dreamed that there would be radios and televisions and powerful jet planes that could fly across the ocean in only a few hours. But all of those things were possible back then even though nobody knew it.

My story is like that. It's about science that seems like magic even today and about the barbaric practice of slavery that so many of our ancestors had to endure.

I'm putting down these words because I'm the only one left alive who remembers what it was like to be a slave in the land of the free, the United States, and I think that it is important for other people to understand what this experience was like.

I made an oath all those years ago not to inform the general population about the science I was exposed to back then, but I don't think that by telling this tale I will be breaking my vow because most people who read these words won't believe in the incredible inventions that were revealed to me by Tall John.

You have to have quite an imagination to believe in his Sun Ship or his power over dreams.

I hope that you will enjoy this tale of adventure and derring-do. But even as you thrill to the dangers and valiant trials of the heroes that lived back then, I hope you will get a little understanding of what it was like to live as a slave at that time. Slavery might be the most unbelievable part of this whole story but I assure you — it really happened.

1.

I lived as a slave on the Corinthian Plantation my whole life up to the time that Tall John ran out of the back woods and into my life. I have no idea exactly how long the time before Tall John might have been, but I was most likely about fourteen years old at that time. Slaves didn't have birthday parties like the white children of Master or the white folk that either worked for Master or lived on the larder of his home.

Slaves didn't have birthday parties and so they didn't have ages like the white people did. Big Mama Flore always said that "White peoples gots as many ages as you can count but slaves on'y gots four ages. That's babychile, boy or girl, old boy or old girl, an' dead."

I loved Big Mama Flore. She was round and soft and always gave me a big hug in the morning. She was one of the only ones who ever showed me kindness when I was little.

My mother died when I was too young to remember her face. Big Mama told me that my mother, her name was

Psalma, had a boyfriend over at the Williams Plantation but she would never tell anybody who he was because she didn't want him getting into trouble for sneaking out to see her in the big house at night.

Flore also told me that that man nobody knew was my father.

"She didn't even tell you his name, Big Mama?" I asked when she would tell me the sad story of Psalma Turner when I was still too little to have to work in the cotton fields.

"No, babychile," Big Mama said. "Master Tobias would'a give a Christmas ham to the nigger tole who had fathered his wife's favorite maid's baby. He'd walk through the slave quarters at night sayin' that he would give the man who looked like Psalma's baby to Mr. Stewart for punishment. So if some slave knew who it was that yo' mama was seein' he would'a done hisself a big favor by tellin' Master Tobias his name. An' onceit Tobias knowed who that slave was he was sure to end up in Mr. Stewart's shack."

Tobias Turner was Master's name and Mr. Stewart was his overseer. The overseer made sure that all us slaves worked hard and didn't cause any ruckus or break the Rules. The Rules were that you did as you were told, didn't talk back, never complained, and stayed in your place.

Mr. Stewart had a shack that stood out in the middle of a stand of live oaks behind the slave quarters. And if you were ever unlucky enough to get sent back there then you were in serious trouble. Many a slave never returned from

Mr. Stewart's *killin' shack*. And those that did come back were never the same.

I hadn't seen Mr. Stewart's torture chamber at that time but I knew about it because I had heard stories from those few souls that survived his torments. They said that he had a pine table that was twice as long as a tall man is tall and that there were leather straps on both ends that he would tie to a slave's wrists and ankles. The straps were attached to baskets filled with heavy stones that would stretch a poor soul's legs and arms out so far from their sockets that afterward the slave could hardly even lift his feet off the ground to walk and he would have to use both of his hands just to get the food to his mouth to eat.

"Yes, sir," Big Mama Flore would say in the backyard under the big magnolia tree that Una Turner's great grandfather planted when he settled the land back before any living slave, even Mud Albert, could remember. "Yes indeedy. If Master Tobias knowed who your father was that man wouldn'ta stood a nigger's chance on the main road at midday."

I was brokenhearted when Big Mama would tell the story about my mother and her sad end. When Psalma died giving birth to me, Una Turner told Master Tobias that I was to remain on her family's plantation for as long as I lived as a remembrance to my mother.

Una loved my mother because of her voice. It was said that Psalma Turner had the most beautiful voice that anyone on Corinthian Plantation had ever heard. Miss Una had a weak constitution and bad nerves and when she would have an attack it was only my mother's singing that would keep her from despair.

Miss Una loved my mother so much, Big Mama Flore said, that she would have been sure to keep me up in the big house with her — if she had lived. But three years after my mother died Miss Una had one of her attacks and without Psalma's singing she succumbed to the malady and passed over to the Upper Level and back to the place that all life comes from.

Some time after Miss Una died Master Tobias named me Forty-seven and told Big Mama that when I was big enough I was meant to live out in the slave quarters and work in the cotton fields with all the other slaves. Master Tobias didn't like me because he blamed my mother for getting pregnant and stealing herself from his property by dying. But he didn't want to sell me off because it was Miss Una's dying wish to keep me on her plantation near my mother's grave.

Until I grew Master Tobias made me live in the barn, feeding and grooming the horses and running any errands that the house slaves had for me. I made myself pretty scarce out there because whenever Master saw me he'd remember my mother and then he'd get mad and look to see if I'd done something wrong. And if there was one straw out of place he would tell Big Mama Flore to get her razor strap and whip my backside. Big Mama didn't want to beat me but she did anyway because Tobias was watching.

After these beatings, when Master was gone, Big Mama would fold me in her arms and apologize.

"I sorry, babychile, but if'n I didn't make you cry he would'a took the strap," she'd say, "and whip you hard enough to draw blood."

"Why he hate me so much, Big Mama?" I'd whine.

"He blame you for his wife dyin'," she'd say. "He just hurt so much inside an' you the on'y one left alive that he could blame."

"But I din't do nuthin'."

"Shhh, baby. You just stay outta Tobias's way. Don't look up when he's around an' always do all your work an' more than that so you don't give him no reason to have me beat you."

We both knew that when I got big enough to work in the fields he'd give me over to Mr. Stewart when he got mad. And Mr. Stewart would use a bullwhip on my bare back. He might even stretch my bones until I was dead.

We both knew that I was safe from Mr. Stewart until I grew big enough to pick cotton, so Mama Flore didn't feed me meat or milk so that I'd stay small and not have to go to work in the cotton fields.

I wasn't allowed in the big house. The only times I was ever there was when Big Mama sneaked me in so I could see how grand the white peoples' lives were.

So I lived in the barn my whole life until just before Tall John came to the plantation. In that time Big Mama Flore made my acquaintance with Mud Albert and Champ Noland. Mud Albert was the oldest slave on the plantation and Champ was the strongest. Champ once carried a full-grown mule across the yard in front of the mansion. Albert and Champ loved Big Mama and so they told her that they would take me under their wings when I had to go out in the slave quarters and live with the rough element out there.

I spent most of my time working hard and avoiding Master's angry attention. But it wasn't all hard work and beatings. The barn was very large and it had a little window at the very top for ventilation. When nobody was looking I used to climb up to that window and pretend that I was in the crow's nest of some great ship coming from Europe or Africa. I had heard about these ships from some of the slaves that had been brought in chains from across the seas and from some of the house slaves who had seen pictures of the great three-mast sailboats in books from Master's library.

I'd sit up there at the end of the day, watching while the slaves picked cotton in the fields, pretending that I was the lookout put up there to tell the captain when there was some island paradise where we could drop our anchor.

And sometimes, if I was very lucky, I would catch a glimpse of Miss Eloise — Tobias's daughter.

Eloise. She was dainty and white as a china plate. Her

pale red hair and green eyes were startling. In my mind she was the most beautiful creature in all of Georgia.

When Eloise would come out to play I'd squeeze down behind the sill of the open window and watch. Even when she was alone she laughed while she played, swinging on her swing chair or eating sweets on the veranda.

Every time I saw her in the yard behind the Master's mansion I got a funny feeling all over. I wanted to go down there and be happy with her but I knew that a nigger* like me wasn't allowed even to look at someone like Miss Eloise.

One day, when Eloise was sitting in her swing chair alone, I stuck my head out to see what she was doing. But I didn't realize that the sun was at my back and that it cast the shadow of my head down into Miss Eloise's lap.

She looked up, squinting at the sun, and said, "Who's up there?"

I ducked down under the windowsill but that didn't stop her from calling.

"Who's up there spying on me?" she cried. "Come out right now or I'll call my daddy."

I knew that if Miss Eloise called her father I'd get more than a whipping from Big Mama's razor strap. He might whip me himself until I was knocked out and bleeding like the slaves I'd seen him bullwhip while they were tied to the big wagon wheel in the main yard.

I stood up and looked out.

---

* That was back before I met Tall John and he taught me about the word "nigger" and how wrong it was for me to use such a term.

"Yes'm, Miss Eloise?" I said. "I been workin' up here. Is it me you want?"

"You were spying on me," she said.

"No, ma'am," I assured her. "I's jes' workin'."

"Doin' what?"

If ever you tell a lie you should know where it's goin'. That's what Mud Albert would tell me. I should have heeded those words before telling Eloise that I was at work. Because there was no work for a groom like me up in the high part of the barn.

"Breshin' the horses," I said lamely.

"There ain't no horses in the top'a the barn," she said, pointing an accusing finger at me. "You're malingering up there, ain't you, boy?"

"I's sorry," I said, near tears from the fear in my heart.

"Come down here," Eloise said in a very serious tone.

I climbed down the ladder from the roof and ran through the barn and to the yard, where the young white girl stood. She wore a yellow bonnet held under her chin by a red ribbon, and a yellow dress with a flouncy slip underneath the skirt. She was eleven years old and pretty as a child can be.

I came up to her with my head hanging down and my eyes on the ground.

"Yes'm?" I said.

"Were you spyin' on me, boy?"

"I was jes lookin', Miss Eloise. I didn't know you was down here."

"Why you lookin' at your feet?" she asked. "You know it's rude not to look at someone when you're talkin' to 'em."

"I ain't s'posed to look at you, ma'am. You's a white lady an' niggers ain't s'posed to look at white ladies."

It was true. Even Fred Chocolate, Master Tobias's butler, was not supposed to look at a white woman straight on.

"You were lookin' at me from up in the barn," she said.

"No, ma'am," I lied. "I mean I looked out but I didn't know that you was there."

"That's not true," she said.

"I swear it is," I said, still looking at my feet.

"Look up at me this instant, you insolent boy," she said then.

I raised my head slowly. I had to look up because Eloise was elevated above me, on the porch. When I saw her face there was a big smile on it.

"Don't be scared," she said. "I won't tell."

My heart skipped at her kind words. I felt as if she were saving me even though it was her threats that I was afraid of.

"Do you want a molasses cookie?" she said.

"Yes, ma'am," I replied.

From a tin can on the swinging chair she brought out a big brown cookie. She knelt down in her pretty dress and handed it to me.

"Now run along," she said. "And don't worry, I won't tell that you were lookin'."

I ran back into the barn and up to my crow's nest. Mama Flore had let me taste the crumbs from cookies before but

I never had a whole one, or even a proper piece. I sat up next to the window and ate my cookie, thinking of young Eloise.

I was hoping that somehow she would remember me and make me her page. That way I could always be near her and eat sugary cookies every night of the week.

That was all before I met Tall John and learned that no man or woman should serve another because that made them a slave.

2.

Time went by and I stayed pretty small. But even still Master Tobias one day told Flore that he reckoned I was old enough to begin the lifelong chore of picking cotton.

"Maybe a few months out workin' will make him grow into a man," I heard him say to Flore.

He told her that the next day he would send Mr. Stewart up to the barn with orders to drag me out to the slave quarters. I knew that I had to go, and Big Mama Flore had spent the night before talking and singing to me so that I wouldn't be so scared. But when that mean-eyed, rat-faced, red-necked Mr. Stewart came to take me I went into a fit of kicking and screaming. The whole time I kicked and shouted I worried that Mr. Stewart was going to take me out to the killin' shack for being so unruly. But as much as I was afraid to be stretched I was even more scared of the slave quarters.

Nothing I had ever heard about the slave quarters sounded good. It smelled bad in there and it was too hot in

the summer and freezing cold in the winter. And every
night they chained your feet to an eyebolt in the floor. The
men out there were mostly angry and so they were always
fighting or crying or just plain sad. But the worst thing they
said about the slave quarters was that once you were there
you stayed there for the rest of your life. You either worked
in the field or you stayed chained in your bunk. And so I
knew that once I went out there I'd never spend any time
with Mama Flore again.

Mr. Stewart would get hold of my wrist and drag me half
the way across the yard and then I'd twist one way or
t'other until I slipped from his grasp. Then I made a bee-
line back for the big house, screaming bloody murder and
for Big Mama Flore to come and save me.

Three times the evil overseer dragged me into the yard
and three times I broke away and tried to make it back to
Big Mama Flore's skirts. The white men who worked for
the plantation were all around the pigsty laughing at Mr.
Stewart, which made him start to curse me.

He grabbed me by the shoulder and shouted, "You little nigger, you better com'on like I say or I'll whip you until you're so bloody red that they'll call you injun!"

I knew he was trying to scare me into being tame but
between the pain in my shoulder and his reputation as a
slave-killer I couldn't help but bolt again. That time I was
so scared that I outpaced the overseer and made it all the
way to the side door of the big house. The door was open
and I could see Mama Flore standing there. I ran as fast as

a wild pig but just as I got to the door Mama Flore slammed it in my face. I could still see her through the little window, but then she pulled curtains closed.

All I could do was to look up at the fancy cloth and cry out her name.

"Big Mama, help!"

I pulled at the door handle but it was latched. As I grabbed onto that knob I could feel Mr. Stewart's grip on my shoulder again. He dragged me off while I was yelling for Big Mama Flore to come save me. I didn't fight any more. I just let him drag me. I was still yelling but the pain in my heart was no longer fear of the slave quarters; I was hurting because Mama Flore had abandoned me like Judas in the story Mud Albert once told me about the man who became like the plantation master of the whole world.

My first moments in the slave quarters might have been frightening if it wasn't for my broken heart over Big Mama slamming that door on me. I had run to her my whole life. When I'd fall and skin my knee or when the thunderstorms would rage in our valley. If I woke up from a nightmare in the barn I could always run to Mama Flore's bed in the small alcove next to the kitchen.

I was an *inconsolable soul* as Tall John once told me that all of mankind was.

"Human beings," John said, "are lost in the needs of their bodies. Most of the time they're hungry or hurting or sleepy or looking for something to satisfy those needs. They're so busy taking care of bodily things that they don't see the world all around them."

But John, and all of his big words, came into my life a little later on — after my early experiences in the slave quarters.

It was afternoon when Mr. Stewart tossed me into the man-slaves' cabin.

"Not one more peep outta you, Nigger Forty-seven," he said, "or I will take you back to my cabin and drive knives into your spine."

This threat cut off my crying for the few seconds that the brutal overseer stared at me. I held back until he stamped out of the room.

The slave cabins were long and narrow like the barracks for soldiers in the army. The one that was to be my new home was made all of wood with twenty-three two-tiered bunks down each side and one feather bed with a pitted brass frame up front.

There were, I knew, ninety-three slaves in the men's slave cabin at any one time. When a man-slave died or got too old to work or ran away or was sold off for one reason or another there would always be a new slave to take his place. It was the same with the women field slaves. The women had one extra rule that the men didn't have — that was female slaves were not allowed to get pregnant. If one did, without Master's permission, then she was punished and sometimes killed. Master Tobias didn't want to care for a slave if she was pregnant and could not work. And he didn't want worthless little pickaninnies running around eating and taking up the women's attention.

Sometimes Tobias would want to have his strongest male slaves reproduce and other times he might want to take some comely slave woman to his bed. But other than that there was no unauthorized congress between slaves or between the white workers and slaves. And so the women had their separate cabin and numbered eighty-nine.

The stench of the slave cabin was unbearable to my spoiled nose. There were the odors of sweat and urine and vomit and general rot. And it was hot in there too. Between the heat, the thick air, and my broken heart I felt that I might die right then and there.

"Well, well, well, what have we got here?" said Pritchard, man-slave Number Twenty-five.

He was the only other soul in the cabin. That's because Pritchard had broken his leg three years earlier and it had healed badly. Him and the slave Holland and some others were helping Master Tobias move a big flat stone from out of the backyard so that Miss Eloise could grow a dozen rose bushes in memory of her mother, the late Una Turner.

Holland and Pritchard, with the help of six or seven other slaves and a mule, had dragged that boulder to the edge of the garden and stood it up so they could let it fall down the side of the small slope there. It was Master Tobias's opinion that when the granite stone fell on the smaller rocks down the hill that it would shatter and make for smaller pieces that would have been easier to remove.

But they used the mule Lacto with a grappling hook to stand the stone up and Lacto must have seen a snake or something down the hill and bucked and ran before Holland and Pritchard could make it clear of the falling flat boulder. Pritchard tried to run but Holland was frozen with fright. So Pritchard just got his leg busted while Holland was crushed underneath the giant rock. You couldn't even see his body the stone was so big.

Master Tobias had been wrong about the stone shattering. It stayed in one piece and so Tobias said that they'd just leave it there for Holland's gravestone.

They called the horse doctor for Pritchard. After he surveyed the damage to the screaming slave's leg the veterinarian advised Tobias to put Pritchard down.

"That nigger's never gonna walk right again, Tobias," he said. "It's no different than I would tell you about a plow animal."

But slave Number Twenty-five cried and begged the Master not to kill him. He said that he could do carpentry work around the cabins and on the house.

"I's still useful, Mastah," I remember the miserable man crying. "Don't do me like a dawg. I's still a useful nigger, you'll see."

Tobias told Pritchard that he would think about it on the ride to Atlanta. He said that he'd be gone for nine days and when he came back he would make the decision of whether or not to put Twenty-five to sleep.

Before Tobias left that rat-faced Mr. Stewart asked what he should do about replacing Holland.

"What was his number?" Tobias asked.

"Forty-seven, sir."

"Save that number and give it to Psalma's bastard when he's ready."

It was the custom on the Corinthian Plantation to give all field slaves numbers. If they got a name along the way that was fine but they would be known to Master and the overseer by number in all of their record-keeping books.

For the first years of my life the only name I knew was babychile because that was all Mama Flore ever called me. Her friends in the big house all called me Baby for short, and if Master Tobias referred to me all he ever said was *Psalma's bastard* with acid on his tongue.

For nine days after the accident that maimed him Pritchard cried and dragged himself around the yard trying to work even though his leg must have hurt terribly. At night he would cry to himself and pray out loud to God to save him from being put down.

Master Tobias came back to find that Pritchard had made himself a rude crutch and a toolbox and he hobbled right up to Tobias's horse and said, "What you want me to fix up first, Mastuh?"

The sight of Pritchard's pain made Master laugh. I guess he thought it was funny how a pitiful slave would struggle so hard to keep his miserable life. Anyway, he let

Pritchard live and in the days after that Pritchard would always say that going lame under that stone was the best thing that ever happened to him. He ate better and staggered around the yard fixing fences and doing odd jobs. And if the Master and Mr. Stewart weren't looking he'd sleep up in the trees on the south side of the plantation.

I never did understand how a man could be happy about being crippled but Mama Flore said, "A slave sometimes would rather kiss the Master's whip if that kept him from feeling its sting."

And so on my first day as a field slave this broken man, Pritchard, was there to greet me, leaning on a crutch cut from a poplar sapling and standing next to a small cast-iron stove. And even though it was a hot day, and hotter still in that close room, he had that stove going. He was holding an iron stick with a rag on one end and with the other end deep in the glowing embers.

"Well, well, well," Pritchard said again. "If it ain't Fat Flore's little puppy dog."

I didn't like him calling Big Mama fat, even though she was, and I didn't like being called her dog either. But I didn't say anything because even though Pritchard was lame he was still a man and I was only half his size and a little less.

"You know the first thing a nigger got to do when he come out chere to the slave quarters," Pritchard said in a loud voice that made me both frightened and angry. "He gots to get his name."

"I ain't s'posed to have no name!" I shouted, and this was true. Master Tobias had said, after his wife Una had died, that I wasn't to be called by any name because I was going to be a field slave and all a field slave needed was his number.

"That was before you came out to here." Pritchard smiled, showing me his brown, broken teeth. I was so scared that I was moving backwards and didn't even know it until my back touched up against the wall behind me.

"Mastuh told Mama Flore that she couldn't name me," I said, not understanding what it was that Pritchard meant.

He pulled the iron stick out of the stove and showed me the bright orange tip.

"Fat Flore ain't out here, boy," he said. "It's just me and you and I got your name right chere on this stick."

When I saw that glowing brand it dawned on me what Pritchard meant.

He was stripped to the waist because of the heat. And on his right shoulder I could see the scars from his branding. Every field slave on the plantation had their number branded on their right shoulder. This was the custom ever since Miss Una's great-grandfather had started the farm. The slaves all talked about how much that branding hurt, but because Flore had never been branded, I assumed that it wouldn't happen to me either. That's because I saw myself as different. I lived in the barn and didn't have a place like everybody else. I saw myself as a kind of young prince in that big shed — like Master Turner's daughter, Eloise, was the princess of the big house.

But at that moment I realized that being put in the slave quarters meant that I was going to be branded just like all the other slaves there.

I shouted "No!" and tried to run away, but the wall was at my back and Pritchard was right there in front of me.

He had been a tall and hale man before his accident. But now he was bent and misshapen as if the damage done to his leg had gone all throughout his entire body. He was light-colored compared to Mud Albert or Fred Chocolate, Master Tobias's manservant. I was darker than Pritchard too.

"Don't do it!" I cried.

He dropped his crutch and reached for my arm but I ducked away and ran off into the long cabin. When I saw that I left him by the only door I realized that I was trapped.

"It's better to come and take it like a man, Forty-seven," Pritchard said in a scary voice. "Because if I have to fight with you, you gonna get all beat and bruised on top'a bein' branded. Take it like a man and it will only hurt like hell."

He picked up his crutch and grinned. I couldn't understand why he was so happy at the thought of causing me pain.

I was miserable then. The numbers on the end of that brand were smoking in the hot air. And I knew that if he marked me I would have lost any chance I ever had to be the prince of my dreams.

"Please don't do it! Please don't do it!" I shouted.

"I got to do it, boy," Pritchard said with that sickening grin on his lips. "It's my job to brand all the new niggers."

Pritchard moved with the shamble of a dead man, taking a step with his whole leg and then dragging the other. He was hunched over too. And he had a smile on his face all the time but you knew he wasn't thinking about anything funny. He moved in my direction and I inched away.

"I got to burn these numbers in your shoulder boy. Got to. That's my job. Here all this time you been layin' up in the barn, huggin' on Fat Flore an' eatin' corn cakes while us niggers be out here eatin' sour grain and strainin' in the cotton fields. Now you gonna know what it's like to sweat and strain and hurt."

"It ain't my fault that they made you work so hard out here, Pritchard," I said. "I din't want them to do that to you."

"I seen you laughin' at me, boy. While I was carryin' them bags'a cotton, while I be hobblin' around on this broke down leg."

He took a step toward me and I took a step back.

"I never laughed at you," I pleaded. "If I laughed it's just because I was playin'."

"You ain't gonna play no more, niggah," he said as he crept forward. "After I burn these here numbers inta yo' flesh you gonna know what it's like to be a nigger-slave workin' sunup to sundown until you vomit up your guts and die."

As he said these words he took a quick step and threw the crutch at me. I tried to get out of the way but that twirling stick got between my legs and I went down. Before I could get to my feet again Pritchard was on me. He got both of my wrists together in one big hand and he lifted me up off of the ground. When he pulled me up next to his face I could smell his rotten breath.

"I'ma burn that numbah so far into you," he said, "that after you die they gonna find it burnt into bone."

He dragged me back across the room and no matter how hard I struggled I couldn't break his grip.

When we got back to the iron stove he dropped his crutch and pressed the iron, which had cooled, back into the red embers.

"Please don't do this to me," I begged. "Please don't. Please."

"I'ma burn you good, boy," was his reply. "I'ma burn you good."

I screamed and pulled and kicked and bit trying to get away from that iron. But try as I would Pritchard got me down on the floor, pulled off my burlap shirt, and held my arms down with his knees. Then he pulled that poker out of the fire and said, "Here it come," and then I felt a pain that I had never imagined a person could feel. It went all the way through me and I yelled and then I passed out for a short while.

I would have rather stayed unconscious but the pain in my shoulder was so great that I woke up crying. I wanted to touch the wound but it was too sore. Pritchard was saying something but I couldn't make it out because the pain wouldn't let me know anything else.

But then Pritchard yanked me up off the floor and yelled, "You bit me, niggah! Bit me on my arm!"

I heard him but somehow it didn't make sense. I was the one who hurt. How could anything he felt be so bad?

"Little bastard," Pritchard said. "Just for that I'ma brand you again. See if'n you bite me this time."

He pulled the brand out of the fire again and when I saw it I screamed louder than I ever had before, or since. Pritchard threw me on the hard floor and then held me down with his knees again.

"Here it come," he said, but the brand never touched my skin.

"Get up from there, Twenty-five!" a man shouted.

It was Champ Noland.

Suddenly Pritchard was gone from on top of me. I heard the iron fall on the floor. I sat up and saw him backing away, brandishing his crutch. Then I saw Champ. He was very tall and powerful with a handsome black face except for a scar that ran over his right eye and back toward his ear.

Champ picked up the brand and put it back on the stove and then he went for Pritchard.

Pritchard was in for it because everyone on the plantation knew that you didn't mess with Champ. He was strong and fast and didn't even know what the word *pain* meant.

Champ moved in and Pritchard swung his crutch. It hit

Champ on the shoulder but he didn't even grunt. He hit Pritchard so hard that the crippled slave fell to the floor and rolled away. Champ moved fast then and picked Pritchard up by his shirt.

"You know it's Mud Albert that s'posed to brand the new slaves," Champ said. "You know it ain't your job."

"But I was just tryin' to help out, Champ," Pritchard whined. "I didn't know I was doin' somethin' wrong."

I almost felt sorry for Pritchard in spite of the pain in my shoulder. He sounded like a lonely child wanting a playmate or a toy. In my mind I could see Champ letting the poor cripple go and walking back to see if I was hurt.

But instead Champ hit Pritchard and hit him again. He kept hitting him even though the poor man was screaming and begging for his life.

"Don't kill me, Champ!" Pritchard cried.

"Why you wanna make that little boy hurt?" Champ asked, and then he hit him.

"Don't kill me, Champ!"

"Do you like it when I beat on you like this?" Champ hit Pritchard again.

"No. No. I'm sorry. I's jes' doin' it to help out. I's jes' tryin' to help Mud Albert out."

"If you evah touch that boy again I will kill you," Champ said, and then he hauled off and delivered a terrible blow. "Kill you." And he hit him again.

Champ beat Pritchard until the lame slave wrapped

himself around the big man's ankles, dripping blood and tears on Champ's bare feet.

I wanted Champ to stop hitting Pritchard but I knew that you couldn't interfere with men when they were fighting mad.

Finally Champ stamped away, leaving Pritchard like a heap of bloody rags.

"You okay, boy?" Champ asked me.

Looking up at him I thought I knew what angels must be. Because even though I was in terrible pain I realized that Champ had saved my life. And having those feelings I began to cry. I thought that a strong man like Champ would be disgusted with a crybaby, but instead he sat down and put his big hand on my back.

"It's okay, boy," he said. "We all cry when they burn us like that. I'm just sorry you didn't have us around you to help you feel bettah about the pain."

3.

Mud Albert came back that evening with the rest of the slaves. Everyone was tired from a full day of picking cotton.

Ernestine, the cook's helper-slave, dragged a cast-iron pot out to the cabin and served us sour porridge in dirty wooden bowls. We were each given a big serving of the foul slop. I couldn't eat a bite of it.

"You gonna eat yo' suppa?" a small man I came to know as Julie asked.

"Naw."

"Then hand it ovah to me."

Julie took my bowl and started feeding himself with both hands. This is because they didn't give us forks or spoons to eat our mush. After all, we were slaves, not civilized human beings.

Mud Albert was the oldest man on the Corinthian or any nearby plantation. He walked with a limp and had many folds in his black face. His forehead was high and elegant. The only hair he had left was at his temples and gray. But for all his age Mud Albert was the most respected man among us slaves. He was fair and deliberate and he never, in anyone's memory, did a wrong thing to another man or woman.

Albert had sent Champ back to the cabin to see if I was there. Champ was to bring me out to the cotton fields but instead he stayed with me after Pritchard crawled away.

Albert and the other slaves came back at sunset, after fourteen backbreaking hours of picking cotton. That's the way ninety-nine percent of the slaves worked back in 1832 — from sunup to sundown, seven days a week, three hundred sixty-five days a year.

When Albert saw my branded skin he took a jar out from under his brass bed. That was his bed because Albert was the head slave in charge of all the other field slaves. It was his job to make sure that we were all chained in every night and that we worked hard and that we didn't run away. For all that responsibility Master Tobias gave him a brass bed that was too old for white people to sleep in anymore.

Albert scooped a handful of foul-smelling paste out of the jar. Then he smeared this glop on my burns. It hurt even more and I yelled out but Albert told me that the lard and herbs would help to heal my shoulder.

After that Albert assigned me to Champ's cot.

The slaves all slept two to a bunk. We didn't have the space for the luxury of our own beds.

Before Albert turned down the lantern he went around chaining each one of us by our ankles to an eyebolt in the floor. They chained us down at night because it was accepted as general knowledge that a slave was most likely to decide to run in the dark.

I was happy to be there next to Champ but it was hard going to sleep with such a big man. He tossed and rolled in his sleep and sometimes pushed me almost out of the bed. But I never complained. I knew that Albert put me there so that Champ could watch over me and protect me from any other slaves like Pritchard who were jealous of the easy life I had before coming out to live with them.

One day, after I had been working in the cotton fields for a while, Mud Albert told me that it went hard for most young boys out among the man-slaves.

"Boys is soft and tendah," he told me. "And men are rough. Boys need a mother's touch, but they won't put them among the women because it's forbade for male and female slaves to live together — that is unless the master says it's all right."

"Why?" I asked in the hot morning out among the cotton plants that seemed to go on forever.

"You'll know one day, boy," Albert said. "But right now you don't have to worry acause Champ done said that he's lookin' out for you and after they seen what he done to Pritchard they gonna know bettah than to mess wit' you."

"How come Champ ain't mean an' angry like Pritchard, Mud Albert?" I asked.

"Because Champ is the biggest, toughest, hardest-workin', friendliest slave anybody done ever see'd. He gets to visit with slave women all around the county and because'a that he don't get so rough."

I counted my blessings that I knew Mud Albert and Champ Noland. But for a long time I forgot that it was Big Mama Flore that made my acquaintance with them.

The morning after Pritchard branded me they had us up before sunrise. You could see the stars shining through the cracks in the ceiling of the cabin as Mud Albert walked up and down the rows with a kerosene lantern shining in our eyes. Then he used his big brass key on each man's leg manacles so that they could get up and go to work.

Champ grunted and turned over, almost crushing me.

"Sorry, boy," he said, and he lifted up so that I could crawl out to the floor.

We went to relieve ourselves in the ditch out behind the cabins. Across the way we could see the women and the girls crouching down and doing the same.

Then we were marched out into the cotton fields for the day's work. Even though the sun wasn't up yet you could feel the heat of the day rising. The air was full of biting flies and gnats and there was the strong smell of animal manure in the mud. It's strange the things you remember. The worst part of that first day was the sharp rocks sticking into the soles of my feet. The only piece of clothing I owned was a big burlap shirt that felt like sandpaper on my skin. I had no pants or shoes or hat to wear. My sleeves came way down over my hands.

Before the sun came up I was paired off with a woman named and numbered eighty-four. She was quite a bit taller than I but not much older: fifteen or sixteen the way white people counted. She'd already given birth to two children by slave men that Master thought would sire strong backs.

Her children had been sold off right after they were born and so Eighty-four had turned sour.

Her hands were rougher than my burlap shirt and I hardly understood a word she said.

Eighty-four had lived almost her whole life out among the slaves in the women's cabin and had nothing to do with white folks except for Mr. Stewart and his cruel work-hands. Me and Champ and especially Mama Flore spent time learning how the white people talked and acted.

To tell you what Eighty-four looked like poses a peculiar problem for me. This is because I remember her in two very different ways. The first was the way I saw Eighty-four as a scared slave boy looking upon a big, angry, black girl. She never smiled or uttered a kind word. She never once asked how I felt or if I needed help. She was, as I said, black like I am black — very dark. And back then, in the days of Negro degradation, white people either laughed at our color or, even worse, felt sorry for us because of our obvious ugliness and inferiority. In my childhood being black meant poverty, slavery, and all things bad. I was, before Tall John came, ashamed of my color and of everyone who looked like me. And so when I first looked upon Eighty-four I was afraid and disgusted.

But when I remember her now there's a wholly different image in my mind's eye. Eighty-four was tall and slender with high cheekbones and large, almond-shaped eyes. Her skin was a dark black that had depth to it like the night sky. In later years I had the pleasure of seeing her laugh many times and so I know her teeth were ivory of color and powerful. Eighty-four was beyond good-looking, beyond beautiful — she was regal.

I know her beauty now, but when I first laid eyes on her she was a fright to me.

"Bes' scurry n' hump," were Eighty-four's first words to me.

"What?" I asked.

She replied by pinching my arm till it hurt terribly and repeated the words, pulling a cotton boll and pushing it into her big burlap bag.

I learned right away to watch her gestures as she spoke. That way I could keep from getting pinched. As it was the place where she tweaked me hurt for over a week.

It was dark when we started but it was hot too. I pulled cotton for a long time, cutting my hands more than once on the tough husks of the pods. I wasn't bothered by the cuts at first because my shoulder still hurt pretty bad.

The moment they started working the slaves began to sing. They sang songs that were not in English and they sang songs that were hymns learned from the monthly service that the traveling Negro minister, Brother Bob, delivered. Bob was one of the few free Negroes in the county who was at liberty to move about. There were a few other freed slaves around that had little cabins. These were favored slaves who got too old to work or were granted their freedom because of some brave act they committed. Usually they saved their Master or one of the Master's children from death.

Most slaves prayed that the Master would have some accident so that they could run in and save him.

"Or at least he could die," many a man-slave would say, "so then I wouldn't have no master to do me so."

Eighty-four thumped me on the ear while I was having these thoughts.

"Dey callin'," she said angrily.

And then I heard it.

"Forty-seven!" It was Mud Albert.

I cut out at a run.

It was full morning by then. The sun was up and five kinds of birds were chattering in the trees. I took the high road because it had fewer sharp rocks. I was in pain from the brand on my shoulder, cut feet, and lacerated hands. It hurt where Eighty-four had pinched me and I was bone tired from the hard work of picking cotton. But even with all that I was still happy to be running in the late morning sun.

When I came upon Mud Albert he was sitting on a barrel in a clearing surrounded by dozens of empty burlap bags. All around the clearing were cotton plants and slaves with cotton-filled bags on their backs that were three and four times the size of a man. The sun was blazing but there was a breeze and I wasn't pulling cotton so it all seemed beautiful to me. I ran up to Albert all breathless and hopeful.

"How's that shoulder?" Mud Albert asked me.

"Hurts some," I said, "but that lard you put on it makes it bettah."

"Good. Now tell me, how'd you like cotton pickin'?"

The question stymied me for a moment. The first thing any Negro slave in the south ever learned was not to complain about his lot to the boss. *How you doin'?* the boss asks you. *Good, mastuh,* you're supposed to shout.

But I hated picking cotton. My hands were bleeding, my back hurt, and there was something in the cotton plant that made my eyes all red and itching. If I told the cabin boss that I liked pulling cotton he might believe me and give me that job until the end of time.

What I didn't know, or what I didn't want to know, was that almost all slaves picked cotton or some other onerous job for their entire lives. There was no escape from that, no chance at some better life. Hoping that Albert would give me something better to do was a child's dream.

As I've said, I was fourteen at that time but I was still a child in many ways. Living in the barn under Mama Flore's protection I hadn't lived much among the men and therefore had never faced many of the hard lessons of life. Because I was so spoiled I still had the dreams of a child.

Children resist slavery better than grown men and women because children believe in dreams. I dreamed of lazy days in the barn and stolen spoonfuls of honey from the table where Mama Flore prepared meals in the big house. I dreamed of riding in Master's horse-drawn carriage and of going to the town where they had stores filled with candies and soft shirts with bone buttons. I dreamed of roasted chickens stuffed with sweet parsnips and onions. And, being a child, I thought that my dreams just might one day come true.

The mature slave knows that dreams never come true. They know that they'll eat sour grain and sawdust every day except Christmas and that they'll always work from before sunrise until after dusk every day for all the days of their lives.

If I were a full-grown slave I would have known that picking cotton was the only job for me on the Corinthian plantation. But being a child I was hoping for a loophole, like a job picking peaches that I could take a bite out of now and then.

Mud Albert smiled because I couldn't answer his question.

"So you don't love Miss Eighty-four and all those long rows'a cotton balls?"

"It's pretty hard, Mud Albert. My hands," I said holding out my bloody fingers and palms.

The sight of my cuts took the grin from Albert's lips.

"I sorry, boy," he said. "I know that it hurts pickin' that cotton. It hurts the back and the hands, the eyes and the heart too. Work can break your heart just as bad as a woman can. Every nigger out here works harder than any two white peoples. That's why I let you have the mornin' pickin' cotton with Miss Eighty-four.

"You really too little to be workin' in the fields yet. I don't know what Master Tobias was thinkin' to put you out here like that. But as long as you here I need you to know what it is to chop cotton. And now that you know I'ma put you out chere as a runnah for the slaves. That means you gonna run heah and theah doin' things for me and the other peoples needs it. So if I have a message you gonna run deliver it. If somebody need watah you gonna fill up the pail and run it ovah to 'em. You understand me, boy?"

"Yes suh, Mud Albert, suh," I said being as polite as I knew how to be.

"An' don't you forget them bleedin' hands an' watery eyes, don't forget the hurt in your back and your chest. Because I cain't save you from pullin' cotton if'n you don't do the job I give ya."

"I run so fast that my feet won't even touch the ground, Mud Albert," I swore.

He laughed and nodded and handed me his water bottle.

That was the first drink of water I had since we got to the cotton fields many hours before.

I know how bad a thing it is to be a slave and I know how terrible it was but I don't believe that there's a free person in the whole world that knows how good a cup full of water can taste. Because you have to be a deprived slave, to be kept waiting for your water like we were to really appreciate how good just one swallow can be. When we finally got a drop on our tongues it was like something straight from the hands of the Almighty.

4.

From Sunday to Sunday to Sunday I ran water and messages for Mud Albert.

Mr. Stewart was the plantation boss and it was his job to organize the work that the slaves did. But Mr. Stewart relied on Mud Albert to direct the workers. No slave ever did anything bad under Albert because he was much kinder than any white boss would be. The white bosses thought that slaves were always lying but Albert was one of us; he could tell the difference between a malingerer and somebody who was really sick.

So Mr. Stewart would sit around talking to the white plantation workers while Albert oversaw the cotton picking, and even the processing of the cotton gin.

All us slaves hated the cotton gin, the machine used to separate the cotton from the seeds and chaff. It was like the hungry maw of Satan himself swallowing every pound of cotton we could deliver. If the cotton gin were idle Master would think that was because us slaves were too lazy to feed it. But Albert knew how to keep the machine going with the least possible amount of raw cotton and he knew to the bale how much the master needed to be satisfied.

And so all the slaves worked while Albert sent me to bring them water and to keep him informed about how everything was going. If somebody was slacking off or else if somebody was sick and couldn't work I'd tell Albert and he'd tell Champ and sooner than you could count to ninety-three the problem would be solved.

There were only two big problems in those first few weeks. The first was my hands. They were all red and dripping ever since my first day of picking cotton. Albert said that he didn't like the look of it but he didn't want to call the horse doctor either.

"Sometimes that crazy doctor jus' say to cut off whatever limb is hurtin'," Albert told me. "An' if'n he cut off yo hands that will be the end of you."

That was all I needed to hear. I carried the water by holding the buckets by their handles on either my wrist or in the crook of my arm and I kept my hands out of sight whenever Mr. Stewart came around to make sure that his slaves were working.

The other thing that happened was that the slave we called Nigger Ned, Number Twelve, died of pneumonia in his cot. Mud Albert tried to take the load off of Ned but by then he was too sick. Three days after my second Sunday in the slave quarters Ned couldn't climb out of his bed. By the next morning he was dead.

Master Tobias allowed us slaves to have a burial service because Ned had been in the slave cabin for many years. Ned was a good man and we all liked him. Nobody except for rascals ever had a bad word to say about him. The slaves all called him that terrible name because we didn't know any better and the white people said it just because they like the way it sounded.

The free colored preacher, Brother Bob, was too far away to make it for to give the sermon and so Master Tobias said that he would say some words.

We all walked to the slave graveyard in the evening after work in the fields. The slave graveyard was situated on the far side of the Master's big house. It was a small plot of land surrounded by a dilapidated picket fence. The slender slats of wood used as grave markers were crowded closely together. I remember that even in death the slaves would never have a place to spread out and rest.

Mr. Stewart let us leave the fields an hour before the sun set so that we could form in lines in front of the grave that Tobias had Champ Noland dig. They didn't give Ned a pine box — after all he was just a field slave. Instead they wrapped him in one of those big burlap sacks and laid him in the ground.

I was standing in front of everyone because I was the smallest of the field slaves. I could see Big Mama Flore standing with the house Negroes across from the grave, behind Master Tobias. She looked at me once but I turned away. I was still mad at her for slamming that door and not saving me from Mr. Stewart. I hoped that she would feel bad in her heart because of the way I ignored her.

A row of jet black ravens stood along the slanted roof on the south side of the mansion. They numbered a dozen or more. The birds watched the funeral proceedings. Every once in a while they made comments in their dry, crackling voices. Back then we saw ravens as an evil omen. Now that I look back on that day I see that it was Master Tobias who should have worried about the portent of those birds.

My hands were hurting terribly. Most of the time I held them up to keep the worst pain away, but I couldn't do that at the funeral. At funerals you were supposed to keep your hands down.

"We come heah today," Master Tobias said after we were all in place, "to say good-bye to Nigger Ned, or as I always called him — Slim."

Tobias, who was wearing work pants and a blue shirt, gestured toward the hole in the ground and then continued, "Slim was a good boy. He never asked for more or complained. We only had to beat him twice in my memory and he always worked hard in the field. You know all the niggers who work hard in this life will have a land of milk and honey after they die. The Lord don't want no shiftless slaves in heaven, only thems that has worked hard and showed that they are worthy of heaven's bounty —"

"Mr. Tobias!" a man's voice called out.

The ravens cried out and took wing at the sound of that man's call.

All of us slaves, and Master Tobias too, turned to see a grand white man on a towering chestnut mare. He had great black mustachios and he wore a black suit with a white shirt. His hat was black with a small round crown and a wide brim.

"Mr. Pike!" Tobias yelled. "What brings you to our neck of the woods?"

Even though my hands were hurting me and my mind was hoping that Ned had been good enough to be allowed to slave in heaven, I was still indignant that somebody would interrupt a funeral and that the orator would stop his eulogy in order to enter into small talk with some acquaintance, regardless of his race.

"I was hoping that you could help me, Mr. Tobias," the well-dressed stranger said.

"Why you dressed in Sunday best?" Tobias asked.

"I like my fine clothes," Pike answered in an arrogant tone. He moved his head around, exhibiting an unmistakable show of pride. His eyes opened wide while he did this and I could swear that for a moment his eyes were like bright rainbows.

As almost two hundred pair of Negro eyes watched, the fancy white man dismounted his mare and sauntered toward Tobias. As he did so he let his eyes wander across the mass of black humanity.

"I lost a slave," Pike said.

"And you think he run the thirty-five miles from your plantation to mine?"

"I don't know," the man said. "Could be. The boy is called Lemuel. He's young, maybe fourteen, and a strange brown color. My wife wants him back. She thinks that he's a healer. But I think that he's just a shiftless ungrateful cur. Et my food and then run like a thief in the night."

"Well, if I see someone like that I'll tell you," Tobias said. "Now if you don't mind these slaves here is hungry and I have a sermon to finish."

Mr. Pike didn't seem too happy with being cut off for the benefit of a mob of black folk. He stood there for a moment too long, staring at Tobias. But he finally got the point and turned away. He climbed up on his magnificent mare and shouted for her to gallop off. With all of that noise Tobias had to wait until the rude visitor was out of earshot before he could continue with the sermon.

"Where was I?" Tobias asked. But we knew it wasn't for us to answer him. "Oh yeah. Slim was a good boy . . ." He called him boy but Ned was nearly as old as Mud Albert. ". . . better than some white men. Take that no good lowlife Andrew Pike. From the looks of him you'd think that he was better than any nigger. But it ain't so. That man right there sold me a horse that he said could work pullin' a plow or a carriage. He took two good slaves for it but it wasn't four days before Dr. Boggs told me that the horse had heartworm. When I complained, Pike didn't even apologize. Took my niggers and left it for me to put his horse down.

"Ned, you can go up to heaven knowin' that you were a better man than that."

Tobias slapped his hands together as if he had dug the grave himself, or maybe it was that he felt dirty having to speak at a slave's burial. Anyway he walked away from the grave and up to his mansion. He left Mr. Stewart and nine or ten men armed with rifles to guard us while we sang over the death of our fellow man and friend.

Seeing those armed men was the first time I ever entertained the notion that white people were afraid of us. As I said, there were plenty of black folk at that burial. We could have overrun those few white riflemen and killed the Master and his plantation boss. We could have taken the Corinthian Plantation for our own.

For a moment I imagined screaming black men and women overrunning the riflemen, beating them with their own weapons and burning down the mansion. I saw the overboss and his men on their knees, begging for their lives like Pritchard had done when Tobias considered killing him. I saw us all sitting in the Master's dining room, eating ham, and putting our bare feet right up on his table.

I knew it was a sin to have these thoughts and it scared me to the bone. I started shivering, fearful that someone could see the blasphemy in my eyes. And if they did, and they told Master, I'd be in Mr. Stewart's killin' shack quicker than they could call my number.

"Are you all right, babychile?" Mama Flore asked.

She had come up beside me while I was having my evil thoughts and while all the other slaves were singing.

"Fine," I said, letting my head hang down and holding my wounded hands behind my back.

"Mud Albert told me that that dog Pritchard knocked you down and branded you," she said.

"It's okay. Albert put some lard on it and it hardly even hurt except if I move." I shifted around, making sure to keep my hands behind me.

"What's wrong with yo hands, sugah?"

"I got to go back to the cabin," I said. "Mud Albert said that he wanted me to clean out from under his bed."

Most of the slaves were singing "Blessed Soul." Flore reached out for me but I moved away and she only grazed my cheek with her finger. She called after me but I just ran, crying bitterly at my sad fate and for the soul of the slave they called Nigger Ned.

5.

Nobody tried to stop me when I ran away from the funeral. That's because I was so small that I was still seen as a plantation child and not of an age to try and escape. And neither did I consider flight because where would I run? There was nothing but plantations for hundreds of miles and if ever a white man saw me he was bound by law to catch me and beat me and return me to my owner.

My hands were hurting and so was my heart as I walked through the piney path that led from the colored graveyard to the slave quarters. The sun was setting and birds were singing all around. Big fat lazy bugs were floating in the air on waxen wings, and a slight breeze cooled my brow. Somewhere in the back of my mind I remembered that times like that were magic and if you looked hard enough you might just see some fairy or saint in amongst the trees. And laying eyes on such a magical creature would change everything in your life.

But that was the first day of my transition from childhood to maturity. Between the death of Ned and the callous manner of Master Tobias I was beginning to see that there might not be magic in the world after all. The man we called Nigger Ned was in his grave with no one to give him the proper words to see him on to heaven. Big Mama Flore had abandoned me and my hands were red and swollen. I was a slave and I was always going to be a slave until the day that I died. Better that I died soon, I thought, before I had to endure too much more sorrow.

It was then that I noticed a sound that no bird or insect could have made. It was a thrashing in the woods. It could have been a badger or an armadillo, but it might also have been a boar or bear or wildcat. I was small enough that a fearsome creature like that could see me as prey and so, even though I had just been contemplating my death, I became afraid for my life.

The fast-moving sound of crashing was over to my right. I decided not to go off the path because I wouldn't be able to move as fast as a wild animal through the underbrush. I lit out at a run down the path and as soon as I did I heard the creature moving quicker still, and in my direction. I ran even harder and shouted once. Off to the side I could see the bushes being disturbed by the animal chasing me. I ran harder but the beast was catching up to me. Then he was still in the woods but ahead of me. I decided to run back the way I had come but when I tried to stop I was moving too fast and tripped over my own feet.

The creature stopped running and I had the feeling that it had emerged from the bushes, into the path. I looked up expecting to see the jagged teeth of a wolf or some other fearsome beast, but instead there was a tall colored boy standing there. He was the most beautiful being I had ever seen. I say that he was colored but not like any Negro I'd known. His skin was the color of highly polished brass but a little darker, a little like copper too but not quite. His eyes were almond-shaped and large with red-brown pupils. He was bare-chested and slender, but there was elegance in his lean stance. All he wore was a pair of loose blue trousers cinched at the waist with a piece of rope.

When our eyes met the boy seemed to be looking for something inside me. He peered closer, frowning and straining as if he saw something familiar. Then he broke out into a broad grin. He walked up to me, put out a helping hand, and pulled me to my feet.

"There you are at last," he said as if we were playmates just come to the end of a game of hide-and-seek. "I've been looking high and low for you."

"Who you?" I replied, feeling like a fool after my fearful flight.

"Yes, sir," he said, "I've searched everywhere from Mississip to Alabam, from Timbuktu to Outer Mongolia."

"You crazy, boy?" I asked.

I was a little put off by his obvious lies.

He just stood there nodding and smiling until a sudden seriousness came into his face.

"Did a big white man with a mustache come around here looking for me?" the boy asked.

"Sho did."

"What did they say?"

"I don't think Mastuh liked that man too much," I said. "He told him that he'd tell him if'n he come across a lost slave, but I don't think he would really."

"Never say master," the copper-and-brass-colored boy said. "Not unless you are looking inward or up beyond the void."

Just hearing those words and seeing that bronze boy made my heart race faster than when I was trying to escape him. There was something about the way he talked to me, as if we had always known each other and now we were just taking up a conversation after a few days of being apart. For a moment there I almost believed that he really had been searching for me. For a moment I felt as if I had been found.

"Are you the nigger that Mr. Pike was looking for?" I asked.

"No master," he said. "No nigger either. No cur or demon or weed. Only life and firmament. Only fire and dark."

All his words became a little too much for my ears. I wanted him to make sense so I asked, "What's your name?"

The bright-eyed, slender boy looked puzzled a moment and then he looked sad. "They called me Son on the Barnes Plantation and Petey in the Lawrence cotton fields. Mr. London McGraw called me Two-step on a Virginia tobacco farm and on the Red Clay Plantation they named me

Lemuel. I've been called a thousand names over the years," he said. "But now, I think, my name is John, Tall John because your head only comes up to my chest."

"Well, Lemuel or John or Petey or whatever it is you wanna be called, we better get off'n this here path 'cause I hear Tobias's dogs comin'. He probably sniffin' 'round for you."

A most beautiful grin spread across the runaway slave's face. He grabbed me by the wrist and, with strength I wouldn't have believed his skinny arms could muster, dragged me through the underbrush and into the woods.

We moved quickly through the trees. My legs were pumping as fast as they could go but it didn't feel as if I were touching the ground with my feet. The slave who called himself Tall John was laughing happily but also as if he was relieved and restored.

We ran a zigzag path through the woods.

"Over this way!" he'd shout, and we'd change direction. "Faster!"

I can't say why I went so easily with the strange boy. Even though he was much taller than I we were probably near the same age. And, like I said before, it seemed as if I already knew him, that we had known each other in another place and time. I knew it was crazy but I had complete trust in the runaway who called himself Tall John.

We moved through the trees so fast that I couldn't mark which way we were going. It felt as if we were flying low like playing sparrows, but I knew that was just my imagination. I was running hard but it didn't make my breath come fast. My legs didn't get tired.

After quite some time of going like that we came to a cliff that looked out over a wide river. Giant herons and eagles flew up above. Down below I could see a she-bear and her two cubs sloshing through the shallow water, pawing the mud for some ort to sustain them in the summer heat. The sun was almost fully set and the sky was red with long black clouds hanging down. A lonely bird cried in the distance and tears sprang to my young eyes. I had never seen anything so beautiful, I had never felt so happy or at peace. I didn't know it at the time but that was my first experience of the feeling of freedom.

"Where is this?" I asked.

"White men named this place Winslet Canyon but the Indians have another name," Tall John said. "That she-bear down there thinks of it as the smell of fish and water with a hint of pine and cougar."

"How far is we from the plantation?" I wanted to know.

"Not far enough," the toffee-colored boy said, and then he added, "yet."

I squatted down at the edge of the ravine and devoured the vision with my eyes. It was so beautiful and serene. I wished that Ned could have been there or at least that he could have been buried there in the peaceful paradise that I never knew existed.

"They're looking for you, Number Forty-seven," the boy that called himself Tall John said.

"I don't hear nuthin'," I replied, not wanting to leave and not caring how he knew my name.

He grabbed me by the wrist again and said, "But they are calling. They sure are."

And then we were running again. Again I was floating above the ground, it seemed. Again I was moving ahead of the breeze. Before I knew it I was on the path and there before me stood Master Tobias, holding the leashes of his six slave-hating bloodhounds.

6.

The lead dog leaped at me and snapped her vicious jaws not a hand's span away from my face. I could smell her canine breath and hear the loud clacking of her teeth biting down.

Master Tobias yanked on his dogs' chains but they kept straining to get at me and Tall John.

"What's this?" the irate slave master said in a voice so frightening that I almost fell down from the weight of his words.

"He done arrested me, mastuh," the runaway slave Tall John said. He no longer sounded like the mischievous child I had met. "Arrested'ed me even though I wanted to run. He dragged me out the bushes and said that you was the mastuh and I bettah heed."

John let his head hang down and his jaw go slack. He stooped over and brought his hands together as if he were pleading. I had to blink at him because he no longer seemed to be the boy I had met less than an hour past.

Tobias, who was never at a loss for words in all the seasons I had known him, went silent and furrowed his brows. He looked from the runaway to me, and back again.

"Is that so, Forty-seven?"

"Yessuh," I said. I would have said so no matter what he had asked. I was so frightened of the slavering, snapping jaws of those hounds that all I could do was nod and say yes and hope that those big teeth didn't tear out my windpipe.

"Who are you?" Master asked the bronze cast boy.

"They call me Tall John, your honor, suh. I was found in a cave near the Paradise Rice Plantation in South Carolina. They speculate that my mama must'a had me but then threw me down there so that the mastuh didn't kill both me an' her."

"You not Andrew Pike's runaway nigger from the Red Clay Plantation?"

"No, suh. Uh-uh. Naw. The Paradise Plantation burnt down and I was on a raft with Mastuh hisself tryin' to get downstream. But he got a terrible grippe and died and I been wanderin' in the wilderness evah since."

If I hadn't heard the boy describe Pike I would have believed his whopper. But as it was I kept quiet because I knew that what was going on was far beyond my control or understanding.

"So your master is dead and his plantation is burned down?" Tobias asked.

"Yes, suh."

"And how did the plantation burn down?"

"I think it was abolitionists," John said, bugging out his eyes. "Abolitionists and maybe injuns too. They burned down the master's house with all'a his family and then took the slaves and run. But I stayed with my mastuh because you know I loved him because he treated us slaves so good."

I had never seen a slave grease a white man like that. The lie was so bold that I was sure that Tobias was about to release the hounds to tear us both to shreds.

"What was your master's name, boy?"

"Joe," John said. "Mastuh Joe."

This brought a smile to the Tobias's lips.

"Joe?" he said. "Joseph. Did he have a last name?"

"I jes called him Mastuh Joe, Mastuh. I stayed with him until he died and then I wandered off in the woods lookin' for a farm to work on and a mastuh to keep me. But I been lost all this time until I come upon Mr. Forty-seven here. I was so scared that I wanted to run but he tole me that you was a good mastuh and that I needn't be ascared."

"You know it's my duty to try and find your master and return you to him, don't you, son?" Tobias said.

The only word I had to hear was the last one — son. When Master Tobias uttered that word to a colored person it was a sign of affection. That meant that the slave he addressed was now his property.

"Mastuh," John said with deep-felt awe in his voice, "if you could bring me back to my mastuh an' his big house I would kiss your feet an' pledge my life to you."

Tobias swelled up when he heard these words. Every plantation master wanted to be loved by his slaves. He wanted them to look on him like their daddy. John had greased Tobias so well that he assured himself a place on the Corinthian Plantation for the rest of his natural born days.

Whatever effect John had on Tobias it was the opposite for those bloodhounds. They doubled their efforts to get off from the master's leash and then they started braying as if they had caught the scent of a wounded deer. Tobias yanked hard on their collars and yelled at them and made them heel. But still you could see their evil eyes looking hard at the both of us poor souls.

"Forty-seven," the master said when his dogs went mostly quiet.

"Yessuh."

"For the time bein' we gonna give this boy here Nigger Ned's numbah and he's gonna sleep in the men's cabin."

"Yessuh."

"You tell Mud Albert that I will call to see this slave up at the big house latah on and that I don't want him molested by any of the rough element out there undah his charge. And I don't want him branded — at least not yet."

"Yessuh," I said for a third time.

But for that solitary response I was speechless. I had never heard orders from the Master like that; for him to be concerned about the welfare of a mere slave or for that slave to be presented to him like a guest at his house. It was beyond my experience. Black men and women were slaves and niggers on the level of dogs to somebody like Tobias. He might come out to the kennel to scratch behind their ears or maybe throw them a bone. But to have a slave present himself at the big house to meet with the Master — that was like a Negro being able to walk down the main road at midday without some white man grabbing him and beating him and dragging him back home in chains.

Tobias pulled on his dogs' collars and dragged them back down the path toward his house. At every step one of the four hounds would turn and growl at us. You could tell that they could feel our flesh rend under their sharp teeth.

"I thought you said nevah t'say mastuh?" I said when Tobias was gone far enough away.

John smiled easily and I could tell that he was again the same confident young man I had met earlier that day.

"When I talk to somebody like I talked with Tobias," he said, "it's like a joke. To me Tobias Turner is nothing more than one of those dogs are to him — just a mad beast at the wrong end of the chain. But when you say *master* and when you say *nigger* you are making yourself his dog and his slave."

"I am his slave," I said.

"Not anymore," Tall John said.

It's funny what one word can tell you. When Tobias called John *son* I knew that he intended to steal him from Pike and keep him as one of his. And when John said the word *any* I knew that he wasn't one of us, the slaves, but something different, something that neither I nor anyone I had ever known had met. I knew right then that the runaway Lemuel, now calling himself Tall John, was something like an angel, or a devil. But whichever one he was I knew that I wanted to be his friend.

7.

"He says which?" Mud Albert asked me.

For the third time I explained what Master Tobias had told me concerning Tall John.

"For this niggah here?" Albert said.

"That's what he said," I answered for the third time also.

"What they call you?" Albert asked the strange colored slave.

"Tall John."

"Tall John? Why ain't they called you Skinny John or Copper John or just John?"

"Tall," John said as if he were considering the word for the first time in his life. "Tall . . . is a funny word, you right about dat.* I mean you could have a tall flea as long as he taller den alla the other fleas. To you an' me dat flea ain't no mo' den a tiny midget but to alla da othah fleas he be like some kinda king."

---

*Once again Tall John was talking like a whole different person. I came to understand that he spoke one way to white people, another way to slaves, and still another way to me when we were alone. In this way John hid his true nature from everyone but me.

"King flea," Champ Noland said, and a few of the men laughed at the outlandish idea.

"So now you want us to call you King John?" Billy Branches, slave Number Thirty-nine, asked.

"I's jes' talkin' 'bout tall right now," John said. "I'as jes' sayin' that if a flea could be tall den why cain't I be?"

"But dat flea you supposin' was taller den the othah fleas," said Number Seventy-five, also known as Black Tom. "I see a lotta men here taller den you."

John's eyes got big and then he rolled them around the room to check out Black Tom's claim. He looked so foolish that many of the men started laughing. I felt a grin come across my own face.

I had only been out in the slave quarters for a few weeks. In that time I had never heard general laughter among the men. Sometimes, before we were chained to our bunks, the men would gather under lamplight and talk in low tones about mundane events of the day. But hearing John brought lightness to our hearts.

"I don't like to conta'dict you, suh," John replied after rolling his eyes some more. "But I done spied around myself 'n I do believe that I am the tallest person hereabouts."

John's outlandish claim brought loud protests from the men.

"Dat nigger's crazy," one voice shouted.

"Dat's a lie!" another indignant man said.

There was a great deal of shouting but as angry as the men sounded they were still having a good time.

"So says you," John said in response to the doubting mob of slaves. "But let me pose you dis . . ." He held up one finger and the whole room went silent. "If you sees a wood barrel stand up to here . . ." he held his hand at the level of his diaphragm ". . . would you call dat a tall barrel?"

"No," somebody said. "Dat's jes' a regular barrel. It'a have to be up to here to call it tall."

The man, Number Nineteen, held his hand shoulder high to show what he meant.

A few of the men grumbled their agreement with Nineteen.

"All right den," Tall John said. "Now what if you see a blade'a grass come all the way up to my chest? Wouldn't you call dat a tall blade'a grass?"

"Sure it is," a voice from the back said.

"Uh-huh," Champ Noland agreed.

A few of the others had to admit what John said was true.

"Now look here," John said then.

He went to stand next to Champ Noland, who was the tallest and broadest man on the whole plantation.

John came up to about the middle of Champ's neck but he was so skinny that it would have taken four of him to match the big man's girth. Everybody in the room could see that Champ was more like a squat barrel where John was tall like a blade of grass.

The men broke out laughing and I was proud that I was the one who found Tall John and brought him into our midst.

But even then I wondered at the many faces of my new friend. In front of the master he was a cowering slave wanting nothing but the master's approval. With Albert and the rest of the slaves he was a wise-cracking joker outthinking us but at the same time making us laugh. When we were alone he sounded like an educated white person from some far-off city like Atlanta or Charleston. But not only that — when we were together John acted as if we were always meant to be friends.

When we were walking toward the slave quarters after seeing Tobias, John had said to me, "I'm glad that we found each other at last, Forty-seven."

"How do you know my name, boy?" I'd replied.

"I've known who you were since before you born, son. All this time I've been doing your job. Pretty soon now I think you'll be doing mine."

"Well," I'd said, "seein' that we's both slaves I guess one thing's the same as t'other."

John laughed out loud and slapped my arm. Then we got to the slave quarters, where he told us about the barrel and the blade of grass.

"Okay," Albert said, finally, after much laughter about John's riddle-like argument. "Time to hit the hay. I'm gonna move Champ over to bunk with Thirty-two and I'm gonna put Number Twelve and Forty-seven in the same cot."

"Why you wanna do that?" Seven, who we also knew as

Charlie Baylor, asked. "Forty-seven and this new boy is small. It'a make more sense to put them with big men like me so we could have some room when we tryin' t'sleep."

"Sleep is the last thing you need, Charlie Baylor. Every time I sen' some'un to look for you they find you nappin' under some cotton bush."

The slaves all laughed then. I could see in Charlie's face that he didn't like being made fun of but I also knew that Mud Albert was free to say anything he wanted as long as Champ Noland was there to back him up.

So John and I were given the lower bunk nearest Mud Albert's brass bed. Champ went around chaining everybody to the bolts in the floor. After a while Mr. Stewart came in to check our chains. All he did was go to the foot of each cot and shake the chains. He didn't even notice that there was a new boy in the cabin.

After Mr. Stewart was gone Albert snuffed out the lanterns and so there was only one candle for light. He took this candle and came to sit next to our bunk.

"Tall John is it?" he asked my friend.

"You bettah believe it, brothah," John replied. His smiling teeth flashed in the flickering light.

"You evah hear tell of the one dey call High John the Conqueror?" Albert asked.

"You mean the trickster from Africa who makes fun'a the mastah an' who means to free alla the slaves an' bring'em back home?" John answered and asked.

"That's the one. They say that High John was sent by ancient African gods to bring us slaves back home to where our mothers' is still waitin' for us," Albert said. "If'n I put high in yo' name instead'a tall dat might jes' be you."

"I haven't come here to free the slaves, Mud Albert," John said, no longer joking or making light. "I came here to find Forty-seven. He has more interest in freeing slaves than do I."

These words made Albert bend forward and peer closely at my new friend.

"Be careful, boy," Albert said then. "You might think you so skinny dat you kin slip through any crack but you can get cut down by the reaper jes' like all the rest."

"I heah ya, boss," John replied, once again smiling and cracking wise.

"This ain't no foolin', boy," Albert said in his most serious tone. "These white folks'll kill a smart-mouf nigger like you an' then sit down to Sunday suppah."

The smile on John's face faded then. But he didn't look scared. It was more like he felt sorry for Albert's fear.

Albert walked over to his bed then. I saw his dark form for a moment and then he blew out the candle, making the room pitch black. After that the men all fell asleep quickly. They were tired from their labors and the cabin was soon filled with the sounds of snores and heavy breathing. In only a few minutes it seemed that I was the only one left awake.

I should have been asleep too. I had worked hard that day too. But I was wide awake because of Tall John. Every day before in the slave quarters was the same. Up before dawn. Work, work, work and then work harder. And then back to the bunk, where sleep came down like a hammer. We never laughed before sleep or had conversations with Master on a country path.

John was something new and this lit a fire in my mind that would not go out.

I wanted to talk to John but I knew that you never woke up a sleeping slave. Slaves needed their rest. The reason they called us lazy was that we worked so hard and we never got enough sleep so we were always tired.

I looked at the sky through the cracks in the ceiling, wondering when sleep would come.

At that moment I heard a silvery musical note. It sounded like a tiny bell and lasted for two breaths. Then John propped himself up on one elbow. He was awake too.

"Let me see your hands," he said.

I did as he bade me, happy that he wanted to talk. I had never met a colored person who talked like he did. Not even the manservant, Fred Chocolate, was as well spoken or articulate as the new boy. Tall John even put Master Tobias to shame with his silver tongue.

I held my hands out in the darkness, palms up.

John traced his slender fingers across my palms and down my wrists.

"The infection is bad," he whispered. "If it isn't taken care of you'll die."

"But I don't want the horse doctor to cut off my hands."

"He won't." John let go of my wrists and moved to get out of the cot.

"Don't," I said. "If Mud Albert sees you, you be in trouble."

"Don't worry, Forty-seven. Everybody on the entire plantation will sleep until morning. A gunshot wouldn't waken them from their beds."

Upon saying these words John reached into his pocket and came out with a metal tube that looked something like a tin cigar. There were red and green and blue beads up and down the sides of the tube that shone almost as if there was a tiny candle behind each one. On the top was a black button like a brimless hat.

"Did you hear a tiny chime?" he asked me.

"I sho did."

"That was my little sleep machine here."

Then John hunched over toward our chains and I pulled down under my shirt. Slaves didn't have blankets in the summertime. If it got cold you just had to use whatever you had to wear to keep you warm; that and your bedmate.

It was never comfortable in the slave quarters; I had always known that. Flimsy walls that let in the winds, chiggers and fleas and ticks biting all the time; no water from the time you went to sleep until the next day when you took your first break from picking cotton. If you were sick the slave boss called you lazy. If you were scared they made fun of you and then whipped you so that you'd be more afraid of them. We were fed sour grain boiled with bitter greens. If there was meat it was half rotten and field slaves never got milk.

Some of the slaves that had come from Africa, or had been around those that did, knew how to steal blood from cows and weren't afraid to eat fat worms and other bugs. But no matter what we did our lot was a hard one. Our hearts and souls were forged in the furnace of slavery and we were made so strong that we dragged the entire nation on our skinny backs.

I felt the manacle around my ankle give. Then John jumped out of bed and lit one of the oil lanterns, illuminating the room of sleeping men.

"What you doin', niggah?" I said to the boy called Tall John.

"Neither nigger nor master be," he said. "Get up, Forty-seven, and fight for your life."

Slowly I raised up and looked around. All of the men were sleeping in the cabin. But it was more than just a bunch of men sleeping. It was like in the late fall when Mud Albert would take his secret fermenting jug from its hiding place in the barn and him and Mama Flore would drink from it and fall unconscious just like as if somebody had hit them in the head with a rifle butt.

"What's wrong with them?" I asked my newfound friend.

"There's a place in your brain," John said, touching my forehead with a long thin finger, "that tells you when to sleep. When there's a certain vibration in the air that place kicks on and you have to stop what you're doing and get a deep rest. I caused that vibration to happen everywhere on the whole plantation with this." John held up the tin cigar.

"All I did," he said, "was push this button and everybody within a quarter mile of here fell into a sleep like the dead."

"Then why ain't we asleep?" I asked.

"Because we're special," John said, flashing a grin.

"I ain't special," I said. "I ain't got no tin cigar to put peoples t'sleep or tricky words t'git peoples t'laugh. I'm just a nigger wit' bloody hands."

John leaned close to me and said, "Not nigger but man. And you are special, Forty-seven. In your mind and your heart, in your blood. You carry within you the potential of what farty old Plato called the philosopher-king."

"Who?"

John smiled.

"Come," he said.

He grabbed me by the wrist, pulled me out of the cot and toward the door. I followed, afraid that Mud Albert would jump up at any minute. But he didn't and we went out into the yard in front of the cabin.

The night air was filled with the chirps and clicks of insects and the smell of night blooming jasmine. The nearly full moon was wearing a cloud as a belt and stars winked all around. I remembered when I slept in the barn that sometimes I would wake up in the middle of the night and look up on a sky like that.

"Can we go back to the cliffs where we saw the bear?" I asked.

"Not now," he said. "It's over ten miles from here and I can't carry you when there's no sun."

Ten miles! I thought that the new boy must be crazy. But then again he did open our chains somehow and I had never heard of the river we saw that day.

"Come on," he said. "We have to go off into the woods."

Tall John had regular Negro features except for his odd coloring. And when he spoke his voice was filled with authority so I felt that I had to go along with him. It wasn't the way that I felt when white people ordered me around. I was afraid of white people, but I wanted to do what John asked of me. I wanted to follow him and find out what he was showing me. Most of what he said I didn't understand, but that didn't matter; I stored it all away thinking that one day it would all make sense.

John led me back to the path where we met that afternoon. We went off about two hundred yards into the shrubs and bushes until we came to a big elm. There was a recess like a cave in the side of the tree and from there John pulled out a shiny yellow sack that was about the size of a carpet-bag.* He rummaged around in the bag until he came out with three small tubes that were like glass except they were soft. Then he returned the yellow bag to its hiding place.

---

*A carpetbag was a small suitcase that traveling salesmen and government officials used when traveling around the country. It was large enough for an extra suit of clothes and whatever other necessities one might need, such as writing paper, a razor, and maybe a little food.

"Come on," he said, and we headed back to the road and then toward the slave quarters.

"What is that you stoled, Tall John?" I asked as we went back up to our cabin.

"I haven't stolen a thing," he replied. "These are mine — and yours."

"A slave don't even own his clothes, boy," I said, repeating words that I had heard my entire life. "He don't even own his own body."

"No one owns their clothes, Forty-seven," Tall John said, "nor their bodies. These things are just borrowed for a while. It is only the mind that you truly own."

"Says what?" I asked.

"And," the strange boy continued, "if no one owns even their own clothes how can they possess another?"

"So you sayin' that Master Tobias don't own his black leather boots?" I asked.

"Every single particle in the whole wide universe is responsible for its role in the unfolding of the Great Mind."

"What's that s'posed t'mean?" I asked.

"It means that if you stick your hand in a fire and burn yourself that you are the one responsible for the pain," John said. "It means that if a man calls you slave and you nod your head that you have made yourself a slave."

"Are you crazy, niggah?" I said.

He stopped and turned, pointed his elegant finger at me under moonlight, and said, "Neither master nor nigger be."

A sudden scurrying came up behind him and I could

see Master Tobias's bloodhounds coming fast. They were bounding at us under a sickly lunar glow.

My breath caught and John turned around. When he saw the dogs bearing down on him he fell to his knees. I figured that he lost all of his arrogance and was now kneeling before the Almighty in the moment of his death. I would have knelt down too but my faith wasn't so strong. I was trying to get my legs to run when the dogs leapt on John. He put out his hands and I thought that they were biting his fingers until I realized that they were licking him all over like he was their long lost mama come home to suckle and love them.

He cooed to them in a language that I couldn't understand. One by one they fell on their backs and exposed their bellies for him to scratch and thump.

"Come over here and meet my new friends, Forty-seven," he said.

"Nuh-uh," I said. "No, suh."

"Come on," he insisted. "These dogs won't bite you."

One of the vicious hounds got up and came over to me. When she licked my fingers I started to laugh. After a while the dogs, John, and I were scampering around the yard, playing as freely as little white kids under the moon-cast shadow of the Master's mansion.

After a long while John bade good-bye to the dogs and led me back to the slave cabin.

Once inside John slapped his hands together on one of

the three glass tubes he stole. This covered his hands with a thick clear paste that he rubbed into the brand that Pritchard had burned into my shoulder. It felt cool against my skin and the pain that still lingered from the burn went away.

John returned the lantern to its place and snuffed out the flame. We got back on the cot and put the shackles around our ankles. Then he gave me the two soft-glass tubes to hold, one in each hand.

"Squeeze these as hard as you can in both hands," he told me.

I did what he said and both little pipes burst in my hands. A cold sensation went through my wounds and I shivered there in the hot and smelly cabin.

"Keep your fists clenched like that," John said to me. "Keep them tight and in the morning the infection will be gone."

I held on tight and John put his hand on my shoulder.

"This wax will heal you," he said.

I was feeling good because for the first time since I had come to the slave quarters I wasn't hurting. My hands and my shoulder felt good and I wanted to talk some more.

"What you thinkin' 'bout?" I asked him in the dark.

"My home," he said.

"Where that?" I asked, "Africa?"

I was beginning to think that maybe Mud Albert was right and that boy was actually an African deity come to free the slaves.

"In a way you could say that," he replied. "I mean *I* am not from there but I'm from a place that is as far away for me as Africa is for you."

"It's even a longer way than Africa is?"

"Yes."

"How far is that?"

"There are many, many miles between you and the land of your blood," he said kindly. "So many that if there was a road from the door of this cabin to the place of your ancestors' birth you would have to walk from sunup to sundown every day for a year before you got there."

"That long?" I said in wonder. "And is your home that far too?"

"For each step that you'd take toward Africa I would have to travel a hundred years, and even then once you reached your home I'd still have tens of thousands years yet to go."

My math wasn't too good at that time. The highest number I knew was ninety-seven. But I knew a big number when I heard it. So when Tall John from beyond Africa said *tens of thousands* I knew that he would wear out the soles of his feet before he would ever see his home again.

This made me wonder some.

"So if Africa is a year away," I said, "and your home is so much more than that, then how did you get here in the first place?"

Again John smiled. "I used something created by my people called the Sun Ship."

"Is that a boat wit' a sun on it?" I asked.

"Not exactly," he whispered.

"What's it like where you're from?" I asked my new friend.

"My home," he said, "is very different from anything in Georgia or anywhere else on Earth. It has red skies and floating lakes and many of the animals can speak and use tools."

"Horses that can swing a hammah?" I asked.

"Like that," he said in the dark. "Yes."

"That's crazy talk."

"Here it is," John said, "but on my world everything is different. People are much smaller and they have skin coloring from green to blue to red."

"Any white people there?"

"Some," he said.

"When did you come here?" I asked him.

"A long, long, long time ago," he said, a little sadly.

"And you haven't been home in that long time?"

Even in the dark I could see that John turned to look at me.

"My home is so very far away that there was only enough power to bring my ship here with not nearly enough to bring me back again."

"And so you cain't never go home?" I asked, feeling sorry for him.

"Only inside my mind."

I didn't know what he meant but for some reason I didn't have the heart to make him explain.

After a while of us being quiet Tall John turned over and went to sleep. For a long time I lay awake looking up into the darkness. As hard as my life as a slave had been I still felt sorry for Tall John from beyond Africa because I knew in my heart that he had come all that way just to find me.

"But what could he want with a nobody like me?" I asked the darkness.

When no answer came I closed my eyes and dreamed of red skies and floating lakes.

8.

I woke up when Champ Noland unlocked my chains. The slave cabin was a terrible shock to me. In my dreams I had been in a faraway land, beyond Africa, where people of every color, even white, lived in harmony and peace. I was there with Mama Flore and Mud Albert and even the taciturn Eighty-four. Even she was smiling and happy in the world Tall John came from. I realized that it must have all been a dream. John never put the plantation to sleep and we didn't play with Tobias's vicious bloodhounds. The strange boy never told me about some crazy faraway home. I was just dreaming.

Tall John was still asleep but when I looked at him he opened his eyes.

He smiled broadly and asked, "How are your hands?"

I looked down at my clenched fists. They were closed around something that was like melted candle wax, only softer and much cooler. I had to pull hard to get my hands open but then I could see that my wounds were healed. The swelling was gone and there weren't even any scabs or scars. A scar in the shape of the Number forty-seven was still stitched in my skin, but it too had healed completely.

I felt a shock all the way down into my chest. Maybe it had all been true: the sleeping plantation, the bloodhounds licking my hands, the faraway home of Tall John and his rainbow people.

"Get up from there, Forty-seven," Mud Albert growled. "You too, Twelve. Them cotton balls ain't gonna fall off into yo sacks."

John and I got up with the rest of the men and went out into the fields. On the way Mud Albert called to us. We slowed down. Mud Albert was old and walked with a limp.

"How's yo hands, Forty-seven?" Albert asked me.

Instead of answering I held both palms out to show him.

"What?" he said, stopping there in the middle of the stony path.

He took my hands in his and rubbed his thumbs over the palms that were red and bleeding the night before.

"What happened to them cuts?"

"I dunno," I said.

I didn't want to lie to Albert. He was a good man and I trusted him. But I feared that if anybody found out about Tall John's yellow sack and healing waxes that he'd be punished. Because no matter how much he claimed that no one could own another person, the Master didn't agree. And it was law on the Corinthian Plantation that anything coming into the hands of a slave was then the property of the Master and had to be turned over to him.

Albert looked into my eyes suspiciously.

"Did Johnny here have somethin' to do with this?" he asked me.

"Wit' what?"

"All right," Albert said on a sigh. "I can see you ain't talkin'. But since you all healed I want you to go down to the east field an' take Twelve wit' ya. I want you t'pick cotton wit' Johnny here the first few days or so. Make sure he know what's what."

"But that's where Eighty-four workin'," I protested.

I still remembered the painful pinch she gave me.

"Since when did a slave get to pick who he work wit'?" Albert asked.

"Since nevah," I said with my head hanging down.

"Den you bettah git ovah theah an' take this joker wit' ya."

"Yes, suh," I said. "Come on, John."

My new friend and I ran quickly from the scowling Albert. I knew that he wasn't really all that mad at me, it was just that he had to show who was boss in front of the new slave.

When I got out to the cotton fields I realized that it wasn't only my hands that felt healed. My whole body felt renewed that morning.

*   *   *

"Don't tell me I gots ta put up wit' you two lazy niggahs this mornin'," were the first words from Eighty-four's angry mouth when we got to her row.

"Yes'm," I said politely, having no desire to receive another pinch.

I ducked my head and grabbed a burlap sack from the ground. I wanted to start picking cotton quickly so that Eighty-four didn't have a reason to be angry.

"Get you a sack too," I said to Tall John.

But instead of getting right to work my friend stood there staring at Eighty-four.

"What you lookin' at, fool?" Eighty-four said.

She wore a faded and torn blue dress that had seen lots of sweat and dirt, little water, and no soap at all. She had probably worn that same garment since she was small and so the hemline was way up past her knees.

"You, ma'am," the skinny jokester, Tall John, said.

"Me? You needs t'be eyeballin' dat cotton."

"I s'pose," John said easily. "It's true that cotton is tall and strong like you. An' mebbe another bush would see his neighbors as pretty. But when I look out chere all I see is you."

For a moment Eighty-four was taken off guard.

"You spoonin' me, boy?" she asked at last.

"Tall John," he said, holding out a hand.

Eighty-four had unkempt bushy hair that was festooned with tiny branches and burrs. She put her hand to a tangle of hair that had formed above her left eye. I was worried that she was getting ready to sock my friend but instead she put out her own hand.

They shook and she even gave him a shy smile.

"They told us," John said, still holding onto her hand, "that we was to come work wit' you. . . . What's yo name?"

For a moment there was a friendly light in the surly girl-slave's eye, but then it turned hard.

"Da womens calls me Fatfoot an' da mens calls me Porky 'cause dey say I'm like a poc'apine. Mastuh jes' call me Eighty-fo' an' I guess dats the bes' I got."

"None'a them names fit a nice girl like you," John said. "So if you don't mind I think I'll calls you Tweenie 'cause when I first seen you between land and sky you seemed to belong there jes like you was the reason they came together."

Eighty-four's eyes widened a bit and she took a closer look at my friend. I'm sure she was thinking the same thing I was; that is — why would he be saying such nice and charming words to a surly and taciturn field slave who was black as tar and ugly as a stump?

"Shet yo' mouf an' git ta pickin'," Eighty-four said, throwing off the web of flattery John had been weaving.

When we came up she had dropped her big cotton sack, which was already a quarter filled. Before she could pick the bag up again. John grabbed it and threw it over his shoulder.

"They send us to take the weight off'a you for a time,

Tweenie," he said. "Me'n Forty-seven here is s'posed t'make it easier for you."

"Boy," Eighty-four said. "Skinny nigger like you couldn't carry that bag more'n ten paces."

"I'll do ten an' den ten more," John replied. "You'll see."

Eighty-four sucked her tooth and grunted, but she let John carry her bag. She and I fell along either side of him, picking cotton balls and stuffing them in his sack.

Eighty-four kept looking over at John, expecting him to falter under the weight of the cotton. We were harvesting cotton balls at a pretty fast clip and the bag was filling up. It wasn't long before it rose eight feet up off of John's back and trailed behind him. But the weight didn't seem to bother him. He was sweating but he had enough breath to keep talking to Eighty-four.

"Tweenie, you evah wished you could jes th'ow off this cotton an' run out into the woods an' jump in a cold lake t'cool off?"

That must have been just what Eighty-four was thinking because she shouted, "Sho' do! Oh Lawd yes. Cold watah on my skin an' down my th'oat. That an'a crust'a bread an' my life be heaven."

I didn't interrupt their conversation. From experience I knew that my presence made Eighty-four angry. So I kept my mouth shut. But I had another reason to keep quiet. I was concentrating on how I pulled those cotton balls so that my hands didn't get cut up and infected again.

9.

Neither Eighty-four nor I carried the cotton bag that day. John lugged the big bag up and down the rows of cotton bushes while we stuffed the sack full.

The whole time John sweet-talked Eighty-four.

"Bein' a slave ain't half bad," he said in the long shadows of the late afternoon, "if'n you could be lucky as me standin' between a good friend and a beautiful girl."

"You should let me carry that sack now, Johnny," Eighty-four said with a smile. "Yo' back must be achin' sumpin' terrible."

And there it was again, just one word. Not even a word but just adding the *e* sound at the end of his name and I knew that Eighty-four was smitten with Tall John the flatterer.

At the end of the day we had pulled more cotton than any other three slaves on the whole plantation. We knew that because Mud Albert kept count.

When we walked the stony path back to the slave quarters Eighty-four made sure that she was walking next to my friend. She even held his hand for a while, making sure that Mr. Stewart wasn't anywhere to see them.

John seemed to genuinely like Eighty-four. This perplexed me because no one else I knew had ever said a kind word about her. So when we came to the fork in the road where the men and women split off from each other, I went up to John and asked him about our work-mate.

"Why you so sweet to that sour girl?" I asked.

"Tweenie?" John said with a smile. "She's something else. That girl could work a whole farm by herself. I don't think that I've ever met a woman so strong or so full of love."

"But she jes' a field slave," I argued.

"That's what you say about yourself," John pointed out.

"But you on'y met her today."

"I only met you yesterday," he countered.

"But you said that you come here lookin' for me. You lookin' for Eighty-four too?"

"No," John said. He stopped walking and so did I. "I wasn't looking for Tweenie but when I saw her I felt all of the pain she feels over her lost children. My heart went out to her. Her loss and mine are very much alike."

"How did you know about the babies that Mastuh took from her?" I asked.

He pointed at me and said, "Neither master nor nigger be."

"Numbah Twelve!" Mud Albert shouted. "Forty-seven! Get yo black butts movin'."

We hurried off before John could tell me how he knew about Eighty-four's babies. I had been with him every moment so I knew that none of the other slaves had told him. But I forgot about that mystery for a while because we were running and Albert was angry and my stomach was growling with hunger.

The men hustled into the slave cabins and Ernestine brought us our porridge.

I wasn't particular about what I ate by that time. Whatever they put in front of me I sucked down while looking around for more. Slaving is hungry work. I was hungry morning, noon, and night. I dreamed about corn cakes and strawberries. Sometimes I would suck on a bite-sized rock just to pretend that I was eating.

That night after a full day of picking cotton I was so tired that all I wanted to do was eat, then sleep. But in the middle of our supper the men started asking John questions.

"Where you from?" Charlie Baylor asked.

"Where we're all from," John said as if that was the only answer and why didn't Charlie know it.

"And where's that?" Billy Branches asked.

"Don't you know where you from?" John asked back.

"I rolled out from a burlap sack on a mud flat in the rain," Number Eight, also known as Coyote Pete, said. "My mam was the hangin' tree. My daddy din't know his own name."

The men all laughed at Pete's made-up rhymes.

"His name was Africa," Tall John pronounced, "whether he knew it or not."

The men all stopped laughing then. I sat up from my bunkbed to see if maybe they were angry with my friend.

"What you know 'bout the jungle, niggah?" Frankie, Number Eleven, asked angrily.

"Not a thing, Brothah Frankie," John replied. "I know about the great civilizations of Kush and Nubia. I know about the blood of kings."

"You come from Africa?" Mud Albert asked then.

"I been there."

"So you are High John the so-called conqueror?"

"No," John said, "not me. But he is among you."

"High John?" Champ said. "Here? Which one of us is it?"

The men all looked around at each other.

"Why, Forty-seven of course," Tall John said.

The men all started laughing, guffawing actually. Mud Albert laughed so hard that he had to get down on one knee and hold his sides.

"Him?" Black Tom said.

"That runt?" Billy Coco added.

"How can you spect us to believe sumpin' like that, Johnny?" Mud Albert asked. He had finally gotten back to his feet. "Forty-seven here haven't hardly evah been off the plantation. Why, he don't even have a proper name."

"Is you High John?" a slave we called Three-toed Bill asked me.

"Go on!" I said angrily.

I was hoping that Tall John would stop his foolish talk, but that wish was not to be granted.

"Sure he is," John said. "Maybe you don't know it. Maybe he don't know it. But that's the way of the Conqueror. He ain't a man'a flesh and bone alone. He's a spirit from the homeland. He burrow down here or there for a while, do his business, and then he move on."

"An' how come you know that if'n you ain't him?" Mud Albert asked. He was no longer laughing.

The rest of the men sobered up too.

"At some othah time High John's spirit mighta passed through me, yeah," John said. "That's why when I see Forty-seven here I can see in him the spirit of the Conqueror. He might not know it yet but this boy is destined for greatness. An' if you stick close enough to him you might jes' find yourself wearing the chains of freedom."

"Chains'a freedom!" Three-toed said. "What the heck do that s'posed to mean?"

"It means many things, my friend," John replied. "And if you follow Forty-seven and you listen when he calls — you might just learn."

"Boy is jest a fool," Sixty-three said, meaning John.

The other men seemed to agree and so they turned away toward their bunks.

Our chains were put on and the lights were put out. When the cabin was filled with snores I turned to John.

"What was all that nonsense you tellin' them about me? I ain't no High John the Conqueror."

"How would you know that?" my friend asked in the dark.

"I know who I am," I said.

"Not if you call yourself nigger," he said. "Not if you call Tobias Master. You have no idea of who you are destined to be, Forty-seven."

"But you do?"

"Yes."

"An' what will I be?" I was afraid of the answer but still I had to ask. The other men might have thought that John was the teller of tall tales but I had experienced his magic. I knew to take that boy seriously.

But that was not to be a night of answers.

"Go to sleep, Forty-seven," he said. "You need your rest."

Those words were like a blindfold being pulled over my eyes. No sooner than he said them I was in a deep sleep. I dreamed that I wore a cape made of redbird feathers and a crown made from broken slave chains. I marched from plantation to plantation and from each one a hundred and more slaves took their places behind me. Behind them the white men who had been our masters scratched their heads and watched us go.

*   *   *

The next three days passed in pretty much the same way. During the daylight hours Eighty-four, Tall John, and I picked cotton as a team. Eighty-four was completely infatuated with my friend. She was always touching his arm and grinning at him. He continued to flatter her, calling her pretty and beautiful even though I couldn't see (at that time) what he saw in her.

They were both always laughing and grinning, except on the afternoon of the second day. That was when John asked Eighty-four about her babies.

"Tell me about your children, Tweenie," he said out of the blue. We were working on our eighth bag of cotton.

"I cain't talk about it," Eighty-four said with a tear in her voice. "It's a hurt in my heart."

"But maybe if you talk about it," John pressed, "then maybe you could stop it from hurtin'."

"You think so?" she asked. "'Cause you know I be thinkin' 'bout them all the time."

John stopped walking and even set down the half-filled sack of cotton. He put his hands on Eighty-four's shoulders and she went down on her knees like I've seen some women do when Brother Bob touched someone, saying that they were now one with the Holy Spirit.

John went down on his knees too and I looked around to make sure that no white man or Mud Albert was anywhere to see. I wanted to keep pulling cotton so that we didn't get in trouble but the hurt in Eighty-four's face made me mute.

"Dey's LeRoy an' Abraham," Eighty-four said softly. Tears were cascading down her berry black cheeks. "Dat's what I named 'em even though I knew that evil-hearted Mr. Stewart meant to take 'em from me. Dey was so pretty . . . an' each time I give birth when I seed LeRoy, an' latah Abraham, I loved 'em so much that it hurt. An' den, when dey took 'em away, it hurt so bad I was sho I'd die. Dey was so young, but Mama Flore said dat dey new master's be good to 'em 'cause dey'd grow up into mens that'd be good workers."

Eighty-four began to howl then and John took her into his arms. I was sad for Eighty-four's loss and I was scared that somebody would hear her and punish us for malingering. And I was also amazed because John was crying along with Eighty-four. It was then that I realized that he felt lost in the same way that Abraham and LeRoy were lost.

The next morning Mud Albert had me take John out to the west field to see if there were any ripe peaches on a tree that the slaves had found out around there. Mud Albert called that tree his private orchard. John and I took a shortcut past the hanging tree.

On the way John was in a good mood. He was talking to me about my future.

"One day," he said, "many years from now you will think back on these days and say that it all must have been a bad dream. . . ."

He didn't finish because when we got close to that tree

he grabbed his head and fell to the ground just as if Champ Noland had cuffed him. He screamed in pain.

"What is this place?" he pleaded. He writhed on the ground and white foam appeared at the corners of his mouth. "Why has there been so much suffering here?"

I got down on my knees and grabbed him by the shoulders.

"This is where they hangs killers an' robbers an' slaves gone wrong," I said. "What's the mattuh?"

He pointed up at the branch where I had once seen Tommy Brown hanging with his neck broken and his fat tongue sticking through dead lips. They hung Tommy for stealing a chicken from the Master's henhouse.

I had also seen Billy Lukas, slave Number Six, swinging in a breeze from that branch. They hanged Billy because Loretta McLaughry, a white woman, had said that he was leering at her as she was riding down the road in her buggy.

John yelled again and then begged me to take him out from there. I did what he asked.

"More than a hundred men have been murdered under that tree," he said when we were far from there. "Murdered."

10.

John, Eighty-four, and I picked cotton for the next days. On my last day in the slave cabin all the men gathered around John because they were used to him entertaining them with some wild and unpredictable talk.

"If you so smart," Silent Sam, slave Number Forty-six, asked John, "why'd you give yourself up to be one'a Mastuh Tobias's slaves?"

"I don't know about you," John replied, "but I ain't no slave."

"You ain't?"

"No, suh — I ain't."

"Den what you doin' pickin' cotton like a slave?"

"I'm pickin' cotton 'cause I wanna pick cotton, of course."

Upon hearing this every man in the cabin, including me, broke out into laughter.

"So that mean if you didn't wanna pick cotton you wouldn't have to," Sam speculated.

"Dat's right."

"An' how you gonna get away wit' that?"

"No gettin' away to it, brothah. If I didn't wanna pick cotton I jes' wouldn't do it."

"But then they gonna beat you."

"That's what freedom's all about," John said in a serious voice. "Free is when you say yea or nay about what you will and will not do. Nobody can give you freedom. All freedom is, is you."

There was no more laughing that night. I could see in the men's faces that they were wondering about John's words. Many of them had thought the same words that he spoke out loud.

I turned in with the rest and went to sleep, not realizing that that was to be my last night as a slave.

"Lemme take this next bag, John," Eighty-four said when my friend reached down to get our next sack the next day. We had filled four bags of cotton already.

"Thas okay, Tweenie," John said as he threw the sack over his shoulder. "Me'n Forty-seven have to go in the afternoon so I might as well tote till then."

"Where you goin'?" she asked. There was the pain of loss in her voice.

"Tobias wanna see me."

It was the first I'd heard of it.

"Mastuh?" Eighty-four asked.

"Tobias," John said again.

"What you got to do wit' him?"

"Maybe if he ain't lookin'," John said instead of answering her question, "I'll grab some sugar an' put it in my pocket. An' the next time they send me out here I'll give that sugar to you for bein' so sweet."

For a second there I thought that there was something wrong with Eighty-four's face but then I realized that she was grinning. One of her lower teeth was missing but it was still a nice smile. The power to bring happiness into that sad slave's face was greater than healing my hands, taming the master's dogs, and putting the plantation to sleep all rolled together.

"You the one sweet," Eighty-four said to John.

I must have been smiling too because Eighty-four frowned again and said, "What you laughin' at, fool?"

Her sudden anger caught me off guard but luckily I didn't have time to speak and make things worse because just at that moment Mud Albert could be heard calling.

"Forty-seven!" he cried. "Numbah Twelve!"

I cocked my head as if listening for more and, in doing so, I was able to avoid Eighty-four's angry question.

"Got to go," I said to John.

"Bye, Tweenie," John said. He dropped the burlap sack and smiled.

She grabbed onto his arm and looked into his eyes beseechingly.

"You come on back, heah?" she said.

And there again was the power of my new friend. We had only been in the fields with Eighty-four for a few days but she was already heartbroken at the prospect of his departure.

I understood her pain. I would feel the same way when John was gone from the Corinthian Plantation. And I was sure that he would be gone one day. I knew in my heart that a person as beautiful and smart as John was not destined to remain a slave on some backwater farm.

But John wasn't gone yet. He and I ran down a rough path through the cotton bushes. Along the way we saw dozens of slaves bent over in half toting giant sacks of cotton. Flies zipped around them and the sun beat down like Satan's hammer on their backs.

About half the way to where Mud Albert was John stopped and looked out at the slaves.

"We cain't waste time, John," I said. "Albert expect us ta hump it."

"I'm just looking," John said.

"Slave ain't s'posed t'be lookin'," I told him. "Slave s'posed to be doin' sumpin so that the mastuh don't have t'beat him."

"I have no master, Forty-seven. No master but the power that keeps my feet on the ground."

"Come on," I said, grabbing him by the arm.

I yanked but he wouldn't budge.

"Do you think that it's fair for those people to be forced to work day in and day out for their entire lives?" John asked.

"We gotta go," I replied.

"Answer my question and we can go."

I could tell that John wasn't going to move until I responded.

"'Course I hate it that we slaves but what else we gonna do? Who would take care of us an' feed us if'n we didn't have no mastuh?"

"You could take care of yourselves," he said. "Buy your own farms, raise your own food."

Nobody had ever said anything like this to me before. The idea scared me. How could I do all the things that white people did? All I knew was how to be lazy and how to work like a dog.

"Let's go," I whispered.

On the way Tall John changed moods again. He made silly faces and did cartwheels as we ran. I got out of my serious mood and even laughed.

When we got to the open field that Mud Albert called his office we found the aged slave sitting on an empty molasses barrel as if it were a throne.

"What you grinnin' about, boy?" he asked me.

"Am I grinnin', Mud Albert, suh?"

"You sure is, niggah," he said. "You an' this red-eyed joker heah."

I thought that Tall John might try to correct Albert's use of the word nigger but all my friend did was smile.

"I's sorry," I said.

"Don't be sorry for laughin', boy. There sure is little enough of it in a nigger's lifetime."

I bowed my head because a tear came to my eye. For the first time I truly knew the sadness of Mud Albert's life. Slaving from the time he could walk until the day we wrap him in burlap and slap the dust from our hands.

I loved Mud Albert and I regretted his unfair lot.

"I got word from the house that Mastuh Tobias wanna see this new boy right away," Albert said. "You ready to go up there, Laughin' John?"

"Yessuh," John shouted.

"Go on then. Forty-seven'll show you the way. He'll wait for you too — so that you don't get lost comin' back."

As we ran between the bright green leaves I asked John, "Why'd you give Eighty-four a name and you still call me Forty-seven?"

Up until then we'd been making our way quickstep through the bushes. But then John stopped and looked at me. His big eyes were filled with sorrow so deep that I felt my heart wrench.

"What?" I asked when he didn't speak.

"Your name is set," he said. "Wrought in metal and sent on a great ship on the long journey across the sky. One day you may decide on another name. But for the rest of time my people and even the Upper Level will know you by the number given you at the Corinthian Plantation."

"What you talkin' 'bout?" I asked. His words were so wild that they felt like mosquitoes buzzing around my ears.

"You, Forty-seven. You," John said. "Didn't I tell you that I've been searching for you all this time?"

"But how you gonna know to look for me?" I asked. "How you even know I was here?"

"I have always known that you would be here one day, Forty-seven. Long before men made iron tools, when terror birds and mastodons roamed the land we knew that you were coming. I waited and wandered and searched until I came upon the Corinthian. I searched for centuries but never once did I give up hope. I never doubted the promise."

"What promise?"

"You, Forty-seven. You are the promise. Your blood is capable of great power, your heart is free from hatred, and your mind dares to consider new ways."

We stared into each other's eyes and a profound feeling passed between us. There was a promise and an obligation that we both recognized. Then we grinned and ran off toward Tobias's home.

11.

"You wait out on the back porch until the Master is through with Number Twelve," Fred Chocolate, Master Tobias's haughty manservant, said to me.

Fred was a tall man, thin and blacker than nighttime. He had great white eyes and a perpetual disdainful sneer on his lips. He wore a black suit with big lapels and a white shirt with a string tie. His shoes looked like black glass they were so shiny and his white gloves made his hands look like cabbage butterflies in a black forest.

Before meeting Tall John I believed that Fred Chocolate was the most elegant colored man in the entire world — the luckiest too.

Fred Chocolate was named by Tobias's wife when she was just a child. She called him Fred Chocolate after a character in a child's book and the name stuck to him. He was such a favorite of the Master that Tobias allowed the butler to have a shack to live in and a wife, Mabel Chocolate, to live in it with him. Mabel Chocolate was also one of Miss Eloise's maids.

Fred spoke for the Master when he was away and even gave orders to the white workers, all except Mr. Stewart. So when Fred told me to go to the back porch I ran around the house to the little platform built behind the slave's entrance.

I sat down on the stoop there and watched the little black ants make their way, in long lines, from the house to their nest under the honeysuckle bushes. Those ants had been making that journey as long as I could remember. Many a day I had sat on those steps watching them, vassals to a fat queen that lived under the ground. I thought that the slaves were like those ants: Flore and Albert and Pritchard and all the slaves on our plantation and all the slaves on all the plantations in all of Georgia. I looked around to see if there was an ant sitting on a pebble looking at everybody else like I was doing. But I never saw a lazy ant. Even they were better than I — that's what I thought back then.

"Hi, babychile," a voice said.

Big Mama Flore had come up behind me and was looking down on my head.

I frowned and grabbed a stick to hit those ants with. But when I was about to strike them I looked down and thought about how I would feel if some hard-hearted person was to strike me and my friends for no reason. So instead I threw the stick into the bushes and turned toward Flore.

"Why'd you shet that do' on me, Big Mama?" I cried.

She knelt down next to me and wrapped me in her arms. I had been waiting for that loving embrace for many a day. When she hugged me I started to cry and she did too. She kissed my cheek and our tears rolled together. She pulled the burrs out of my hair.

She didn't answer my question but it wasn't necessary. In my heart I knew why she turned me away. I had to be a field slave if that was what Tobias wanted. I had to do what the Master decreed.

Neither master nor nigger be, the words came to me as they would time and again over the many years of my long life. John had given me a gift that was also a danger if I ever said it out loud.

"How's it goin' out there with Mud Albert and Champ?" Flore asked me.

It was just a simple question. One word would have sufficed for the answer. But it opened the floodgates of my pain and labor. I told Flore about Pritchard branding me and about Champ's beating of him. I told her about the cotton and Eighty-four's pinches and the chiggers and biting gnats, I talked about Tall John but I didn't tell her about the wonderful things he could do. I didn't tell because I was worried that if Master knew about John's powers he might take him away and I'd never see him again.

"Lemme see yo hands," Flore said at one point.

I held up my palms.

"They all healed," she said. "Mud Albert said that you had real bad cuts. How'd they get bettah?"

I hunched my shoulders. I really didn't know what John had done.

"I guess I jes heal quick," I said.

We talked for a long time and at the end Flore wrapped four molasses cookies in a napkin that she pinned to the inside of my work shirt. Not long after that Fred Chocolate showed up with Tall John in tow.

"Go back to work," the haughty manservant said.

Flore kissed my cheek. Then she looked at my new friend and said, "So you the new boy?"

"Yes ma'am," John said brightly.

"My baby here likes you," she added.

"He is a fine person, Number Forty-seven is," John answered. "The finest the human race has to offer."

"Watch your mouth," Fred Chocolate said as he slapped the top of John's head.

But my friend didn't cower or wince. He kept Flore's eye and she looked at him in wonder and maybe even with a little fear.

"It was nice to meet you, young man," she said then.

"I'm afraid you'll be seein' more of him than you want to," Fred said. "Mastuh seems to think that this copper-colored piece'a trash can help Miss Eloise."

"He has the touch?" Flore asked.

"Mastuh think so."

"Do you?" Flore asked John.

"My people know a great deal about herbs and healing," he said. "We've been curing disease for longer than even we can remember."

"That's the lies he tole Mastuh," Chocolate said. "Now we have to smell his field stink all over our house."

I heard all the words but I didn't really care about anything but the insinuation that Miss Eloise was sick.

Back then in my *slavemind,* as John called it, I thought that Eloise was the closest thing you could come to an angel here on Earth. She was to me the most beautiful girl in all the world. I loved her in my heart as Brother Bob told us we had to love the Lord. Every night when I remembered to say my prayers I asked Him to keep her safe. I felt that if anything happened to Miss Eloise that I would die too.

Eloise was a beautiful child, that's for sure. And I learned later that she was a good person too. But now I realize that I loved her whiteness when I was still a slave because that whiteness meant freedom, and freedom was what I wanted more than anything in the world — even though I didn't know it.

As soon as John and I were away from the back door of the mansion I asked him, "Did you see Miss Eloise?"

He didn't answer me right off. Instead he walked with me in silence until we got to a fence behind the chicken coop. We climbed up and over the few rungs and went maybe a dozen paces into the bushes. There, behind a big bramble bush, was a downed cottonwood tree that made a perfect seat for someone who needed to take a load off without being seen. I had never known about that resting place and I wondered how John knew to walk right to it. But I was too upset about Miss Eloise to question him about it.

"Did you see her?" I asked again.

John sat back on the cottonwood trunk and pulled his knee up to his skinny chest.

"Yes, I did," he said after a moment's thought. "Tobias asked me if I knew anything about healing. He said that Andrew Pike said that his wife thought that the runaway slave was a healer. I told him that I wasn't Pike's runaway, even though I am, and he said that I didn't have to worry about Pike, that Pike owed him two slaves and so that I was safe with him. All he cared about was if I was a healer."

"And what did you say?" I said, trying to move the story along.

"I told him that my people knew about healing."

"And so? Did you see Miss Eloise?" I asked for the third time.

"Yes. Tobias brought me to her. Her room is filled with sunlight. It was brightly painted and the windows were open. But she had bad color and was sleeping badly. She had fever."

"What's wrong with her?" I cried.

"I was only allowed to take her pulse," John said. "But I'm pretty sure that she has a blood infection. It seems to have gone to her brain."

"Naw it ain't," I cried, putting my hands to my head. "I just saw her last week swinging on the swing in the garden with her girlfriends."

"She was probably already sick but it was only since then that the infection entered her brain."

"Don't say that!" I yelled. I didn't want to hear something that might cause the beautiful Miss Eloise to die.

"We have to go looking for herbs," John said, not seeming to be very concerned. "Tobias gave us permission to wander around the woods here gathering the medicines they think we'll need to save her life."

With that John got up and strode off into the woods. I followed him, somehow realizing that these were the first steps to an education that would take me I knew not where.

12.

As soon as we were off the path John took me by the wrist and again we ran on the wind — over boulders and through thick bushes, past trees that were ancient giants looming over dark forest undergrowth.

At one point we came to a field of wild strawberries. John stopped there and took off his new/old work shirt to gather the berries for our lunch. It was then that I remembered the molasses cookies Flore pinned to my shirt. We sat down on the grass and ate for a while. I was worried about Eloise but I was hungry too. Ever since I had been working in the fields I was hungry all the time, nearly starving. I wanted to help Eloise but I couldn't turn down a meal.

John told me that the forest we were in was very old and filled with spices and fungi that were wonderful for the human anatomy.

"What do gnats got to do wit' men?" I asked, trying to put together the strange sounds he uttered.

"Not *gnat man*," he said. "Human anatomy. That is the study of the parts of the human body."

"Who told you about *gnat man me*?"

Tall John smiled and put a hand on my shoulder.

"I am not what I appear to be," he said. "I come from far, far away as I have already told you. This body of mine, though completely human, was created by what my people call science. Because of this I have a great deal of knowledge about the human body. I know all of the mechanics — it is only the human heart that I fail to understand."

"And do you know what mushrooms will get the bugs outta Miss Eloise's brain?" I asked, unconcerned with his silly notions.

"Yes," he said. "There are a few herbs that will assist her healing. And also you need proper rest and nutrition after that infection in your hand and the burn on your shoulder. You need sustenance."

"I don' care about me," I said. "I just wanna make sure that Miss Eloise gets bettah. An' you shouldn't lie to the Master —"

John held up a finger and I knew that he wanted me to remember his admonition.

"It don't mattah if you call'im Master or Tobias," I continued. "If he figures out that you jes' wanna run around an' eat strawberries he'll put you in the killin' shack and that will be all she spoke about you."

John smiled and said, "You love that little child Eloise don't you, Forty-seven?"

"She's like the angels that Brother Bob talks on and on about at his sermons."

"She's just a person."

"No," I complained. "She's the most beautiful girl in the world."

"Eighty-four is just as beautiful in her own way," my new friend argued.

"How can you say somethin' like that, boy?" I said. "Eighty-four's black and ugly with nappy hair and liver lips. She couldn't even hold a candle to Miss Eloise."

"Come with me," Tall John said.

He jumped up from where we were and led me a short way down an animal path to a wide, still pond.

"Look," he said. "Look at yourself in the water."

The water was absolutely motionless and reflective like a polished mirror. I could see my whole image from head to toe.

"Take off that shirt, Forty-seven."

I did as he told me, standing naked at the pond's edge.

When I looked down into the reflective pool I could see that my skin was very dark and that my body was like a man's but smaller. My hair was wild and every which way, but I looked like I imagined myself.

"You have a perfect face and body and the strength to run all day without aches and pains," John said. "You have big, inquisitive eyes and a heart that's open to the pain of others. You love Eloise and so she is beautiful to you, but Eighty-four needs your love too. And if you gave it to her you would see her beauty even as you see it in the white child."

"But beauty just is," I said. "I can't make somethin' lovely jes' by sayin' so."

John waved his hand and my image in the pond changed into Big Mama Flore. She was just sitting there shelling peas and throwing them into a basket. My heart opened up when I saw Flore.

"Is she beautiful?" John asked.

"Oh, yes," I cried. "She's the most beautiful thing in all the world."

"She has black skin and nappy hair," John argued. "She has big lips and ashy elbows."

I turned away from the image in the water and asked, "Are you a angel?"

"No, Forty-seven. I'm just a helper."

"What you helpin'?"

"I'm helping you to save the universe."

"But I'm just a nig —" I stopped myself in the middle of the prohibited word.

"All of my people," John said, "my whole race says a prayer for you every night. They have given you their blessings and their hope. A black-skinned, nappy-headed child who was born into slavery and who shall ride into the greatest battle in the history of the world."

When Tall John from beyond Africa spoke I almost believed what he said. There was so much confidence in his tone that you were compelled to believe him.

I took a deep breath and felt the weight of his words on my shoulders. I didn't even know where Universe was, or how big it was. I figured that it must have been at least as big as Georgia, and Georgia, I knew, was so big that it would take a strong man three weeks to walk from one end to the other.

"Boy, what you yammerin' about?" I asked. "I'm just a nigger, born a slave."

"No," John said. "You are Forty-seven. You are the hope of your world and mine — and all that lies between."

"You is crazy, boy."

Instead of answering John laughed and pushed me into the pond. The shock of the cold water and of peaceful John pushing me made me laugh so hard that I couldn't climb out again. But then John held out his hand and made like he was going to help me. But the minute I pulled against him he pushed me in again. He stood there at the water line laughing at me.

"Help me out, fool," I said.

And when he stuck out his hand I grabbed on and let my weight go, pulling him in with me. He started sputtering and trying to jump out of the pond. But every time he got his footing I pushed him back again. We were laughing so hard that finally we climbed up to the shore and fell down in the mud.

That was one of the happiest moments I've had in the nearly two hundred years of my long life here on Earth. Before that day I never knew what it was to laugh without worrying that somebody might hear and come and thump my head. I never knew what it was like to lie there next to your best friend in the whole world and not have a care.

I had eaten strawberries and cookies and went splashing in a forbidden pond.

It was forbidden because all things that were fun or free were forbidden to slaves. I didn't know exactly who owned those strawberries but one thing for sure — it was a white man.

But none of that mattered because there I was, alone in the woods with the most wonderful person I had ever known. When he looked at me he liked my black skin and dusty hair, he thought that I was a hero and who was I to say no?

After a long while lying in the mud I waded out into the water to wash my skin and rough blouse. When we were ready to go John looked up at the sky and scowled.

"Clouds," he said. "We may have to find shelter."

Him saying the word *shelter* reminded me of something.

"How did you know where that tree trunk where we sat down on was?" I asked. "I mean you walked right to it just like you knew it was there."

"You see, Forty-seven?" he said as if I had just proven a point. "You notice things and you don't only notice but you ask why. Those are only two of the reasons why you are destined to become a great hero."

"You ain't answered my question, John."

"I've been hanging around the plantation for almost a week," he said. "Looking for you."

"Me?"

"I could sense you, hear your music among all of the music that men make with their blood."

"Music in they blood?" I said, suddenly afraid that John might be some kind of devil that drinks men's blood.

"Yes," he said with a smile. "Every living being has their own song thrilling through the strings that hold them together. I knew your song. I just had to make sure I really heard it playing in amongst the others. And once I knew you were here I had to meet you to make sure that you were up to the task."

"What task?"

"Saving the universe."

"Where's that?"

"Everywhere," he said, "all over the world and up to the stars."

"Like a ocean?"

"Something like that," John said.

"If you was free an' lookin' fo' me den why'd you let 'em make you into a slave?" I asked.

"Because of a creature named Wall," John said seriously.

"Who's that?"

"He's the one who might destroy everything unless we stop him. He found out that I had been on the Red Clay Plantation —"

"What was you doin' there?"

"Looking for you. All I have done for the past three thousand years is look for you. That's because I knew *that* you would be but I didn't exactly know *where* and *when*. That's why I was on the Red Clay Plantation, because someone with a song almost like yours was there. But when I realized that it wasn't you I ran away. After I left Wall caught my scent and he took over Andrew Pike's body and came looking for me."

"And so Andrew Pike is under a spell?"

"Pike is dead and Wall walks the earth in his flesh."

"And who is this Wall?"

"He is, as far as you are concerned, the devil."

These words shook me to my soul. I didn't want to ask any more questions. I didn't want John to tell me any more.

Again he looked at the sky.

Again he said, "Clouds."

"Maybe it'll rain," I said, grateful for mundane conversation. "That'll be good for the gardens."

"But I can't carry you if the sun isn't out."

"Why not?"

"Because my powers, such as they are, are derived from solar energy. My body is like a battery that converts power of the sun into action. If I were to attempt to carry us home without the sun shining my energy would run out and I might even die."

"How far is we from Corinthian?" I asked.

"Sixty miles at least."

Before I could voice my dismay John grabbed me by the wrist and we took off. We ran for a short time and finally came to one of the big trees we'd passed earlier. Fat raindrops had started to fall and the sky was dark with rain clouds.

"We'll have to stay here until the sun comes out again," John said.

"What if it don't come out?" I asked.

"Then we will have to wait until morning."

"Mastuh'll kill us we do that," I wailed.

"As long as you see him as master he may very well," John said. "But if you see that you and he are equals and you realize that he needs you more than you need him then, just maybe, you will be reprieved."

My heart was beating fast and my guts were churning.

"Let's try to run back," I cried.

"It's at least thirty miles away, Forty-seven, maybe forty. We would never make it in time."

"But he'll kill us."

"Kill us and he kills his precious Eloise."

I wanted to beat the smug slave's face in. Here he had shown me the best time of my whole life and now he was going to get me killed. Why did I ever go with him?

The rains came down hard but the thick foliage of the ancient tree kept us mostly dry. The ground was mulched pretty well by dead leaves and so the space was like a big, carpeted room. When the night came on it became very dark. John and I leaned against the bark, shoulder to shoulder. The dark and the sound of the rain, and maybe the fear of Tobias, made me very tired. I nodded and almost fell asleep.

"Do you want to see where I'm from?" I thought I heard him say.

"Might as well," I said, "seein' as it'll prob'ly be the last story I hear 'fore Mastuh tie me to that wagon wheel an' have 'em whip me till I'm dead."

I turned on my side and I'm pretty sure that I fell asleep.

13.

I opened my eyes on a beautiful day in some far-off and wonderful place. Not only was I awake but I was running down an open road.

Somewhere in my mind I worried that I might be seen by some white man who would beat me like the slave laws demanded. I worried, but the road was broad and straight so I figured that if I saw somebody coming that I could run away before they could catch me and bring me back to the plantation.

But when I looked around I realized that I didn't need to worry. The plants on the side of the road were red and purple, without leaves, not at all like proper trees. And the sky was pink and red and the road was paved with something like glass, and there was no sun in the sky but it was still bright and clear.

"This is where I am from," a voice said.

I stopped running and turned to see my friend was standing there next to me.

It was John and then again it wasn't. He had the same

voice and his eyes were deep and kind as they had been on the Corinthian Plantation. But in this new place he was a head taller, quite a bit thinner, and his skin was more orange than brown. And above his head I could see a shimmering light that moved when he did.

You can imagine that I was amazed by the events unfolding around me. The last thing I remembered was being under a tree in a rainstorm. Now all of a sudden I was in a strange new land and my friend had grown a foot and changed colors on me.

"What the hell you doin' to me, niggah?" I said.

He pointed at me and said, "Neither master nor nigger be."

In this new place his words took on a new meaning. They brought about a vision: I saw Tobias and the cowering Pritchard in my mind. The slave master was holding a whip and the abject slave was writhing on the ground, begging our master for mercy.

I didn't want to be either one of them. I reached out in my imagination and pushed their images away. Then I turned my attention back to Taller John and his lecturing finger.

"That's right, Forty-seven," John said as if he knew what had been going on in my head, as if he saw the tableau of master and slave in my mind.

"Go beyond it," John continued. "Just because they treat you like that doesn't mean that you have to believe in them."

As the images faded from my mind I was once again aware of the strange land around me.

"You live here?" I asked.

"No," Tall John, the orange being from beyond Africa, said.

"But you were born here?"

"Yes," he said. "My ancestors were born here many millions of years ago. It is a planet called Elle and it is so far from Earth that it is as if it doesn't really exist."

"Far beyond the dirt?" I asked. The only time I had heard anyone use the word *earth* they were talking about the soil beneath our feet.

"Earth," he said again. "It is the planet you come from. Like the moon only larger and crowded with life."

"An' this place —"

"My planet — Elle," he interjected.

"Yeah. This place Elle is a earth too but so far away that you cain't get there?"

Tall John nodded and smiled. He was even taller now and his orange skin was tinged with purple. The light above his head brightened and I was beginning to think that he wasn't a boy at all.

"An' why couldn't we bring our real bodies here?" I asked.

"Because if I spent the rest of my life trying to get here I would hardly be any closer than I am now under that tree in my sleep."

"You as far from yo home as I am from my freedom," I said, surprising myself with the thought.

John smiled and nodded. He put his hand on my shoulder and we walked on in the strange landscape.

As we walked he spoke to me in his commanding tone.

"But I could bring us here because all I have to do is remember and the great mind delivers me."

"Like if I remembered the river you brought me to?" I asked. "I could go there just by rememberin' it?"

"Yes," John said. "Behind all of existence there is one great mind. And every single living, thinking being is a part of that mind. Once you learn to connect with it you can always return to a place or a thought that you once had."

"Like make-believe?" I asked.

"No. We are really here at this moment but as wraiths."

"Ghosts?"

"Someone ignorant of the Great Mind might see us as ghosts but no one on Elle would make that mistake."

As we walked the red and purple forest gave way to a wide plain made up of what looked like piles of stones. The stacks of rock were gray and red-brown and none were piled higher than a man. The piles were all shivering. They looked like rock-studded cocoons ready to release their butterflies.

"That's right," John said as if he could hear my thoughts. "They are living things, creatures of the Calash."

"These are your people?" I asked.

"No," the taller and taller boy said. "Not really. I mean, once we were all one people but that was so long ago that there are very few records that survive to document our relationship."

As he spoke one of the shivering piles of stones exploded outward, disgorging an albino creature that was made up of a great head, from which hung a dozen limbs that seemed to work as both legs and arms. The creature (which was about the size of a wild boar) climbed to the top of a nearby pile and shook itself, throwing off the water of its birth. Then it moved its head around until great blue wings sprouted from the back. The beautiful creature let out a terrible scream and then flew aloft on its blue wings.

"Where's it goin'?" I asked as my friend and I watched the winged thing fade into the pink-and-red horizon.

"To seek the God-Mind and kill it," he said. "To rend the universe open and feast on its heart."

Up until that moment I wasn't truly troubled by the sights I beheld. Even the physical changes to John's body didn't seem so strange to me. I already knew he was different on the inside from the way he talked. But John's words about destruction set off a deep agitation in my heart. I had no idea what a God-Mind was but I had heard the word *God* before and I knew that killing was bad no matter who it happened to.

The stacks of birthing stones spread out as far as the eyes could see. Here and there albino members of the

Calash race were rising up from their cocoons and taking flight.

"There must be more of'em than Mud Albert could count," I said.

"They are as plentiful as the stars," John agreed, "and yet there is but one."

"What's that mean?" I asked.

"You will see," he said.

Another stack of stones burst open — nearer to us. The big-headed white creature with its dozen limbs crawled out and shifted and turned until it had wings. But this one, rather than gliding off into the sky, turned its one great black eye upon my friend and me. The creature screamed as did the previous newborn, but instead of leaving he dove at us. John and I ducked down to keep from being battered by those blue wings. As we arose the eerie bird-like thing wheeled in the sky, obviously intent on attacking again.

"Let's skip this part," John said.

He waved his orange and purple hand through the air and suddenly we were standing on a black platform in a wide, glassy sphere. There was no sky above or ground below us, only thousands of small black platforms that jutted out from the sides of the globe. When I looked around the sphere I realized that we were in the largest place that I had ever been, even larger than that valley where I saw the she-bear and first imagined being free.

While I watched, a small creature walked out up the ledge nearest my eye. He was no larger than a baby chick but the same proportions as tall, lean John. He was bright yellow in color and when he saw my face he smiled and nodded. The light above his head lengthened like a candle reaching its highest flame.

"Hello, hero," he said.

"My name ain't hero, it's Forty-seven, but hello to you too, little yellah man."

As I spoke these words I noticed tiny little men and women were climbing out onto the thousands of ledges around me. They were every different color of the rainbow and all of them so bright that the big sphere got as clear as midday.

"Who are all these little people?" I asked.

"They are my people," Tall John said in my ear.

I turned to ask how we got from one place to the other. But as I did so I found myself facing another small ledge, and on that ledge I saw a tiny little Tall John standing there and smiling.

"Is this what you really look like?" I asked.

"Yes," he said.

"And is this your home?"

"This is Talam the primal hive," small Tall John said. "It is where we fled when the Calash tried to steal our technology and use it to tear open the fabric of the world."

I had no idea what his words meant but I knew that it couldn't be good.

"As I told you before, there is a higher place," John said.

"The Great Mind," I added.

"That's right. It is the place where all mind resides. You are there and I am too, but we are also in the physical world with our bodies and with each other. In the physical world every being is different, but there, in the higher place, we are all the same."

I didn't know what he meant by all that. It sounded like when Brother Bob would deliver a sermon but here there was no podium or cross. Without those things to secure my eyes I realized that I had never understood those sermons.

"And so you and them Calash things are really the same?" I asked.

"Yes," my diminutive friend said, "and no. In the upper reality we are all the same, flowing in one direction, with one eternal plan. But here in the material world the Calash believe that they can break the barrier between mind and matter and feast upon the pure energy of the God-Mind."

"And that's bad?"

"They will never succeed, but in trying to do so they could throw the whole universe into turmoil. They will never be able to conquer the walls of heaven as they wish, but they can destroy all life and therefore strangle the spirit until it is warped out of all understanding."

All around me thousands of thousands of tiny bright-colored men and women began to weep.

"What do you want me to do?" I asked, intent upon helping those wee folk if I could.

It was the most important decision of my long life and I didn't even stop to think about it. Tall John, my first true friend, said that there was a battle brewing between him and the wing-heads called the Calash. Well, then, I would do what I could to defend my friend and the universe — whatever that might be.

There came a tittering among the uncountable elfin citizens of the great hive. Then they all cheered. They had small voices but there were so many of them that the sound came like a roar.

"I told you," John said, addressing the unlikely congress of elves. "I told you that he was the one."

"But will he have the ability to stand against Wall?" a thousand voices asked.

"Victory can never be assured," John replied. "But at least he is willing."

"You could destroy the planet," a thousand thousand voices bellowed. "Destroy Earth and Wall will die."

"How would we be able to distinguish ourselves from the Calash if I were to do such a thing?" John's single voice asked. "There are plants and fish and insects . . ." at each mention of a life form the image appeared before the great congregation. And every time the little people beheld the beauty of life on Earth they tittered and cooed. ". . . there are men and bears and eagles flying," John continued, "and we will not end them because that would mean that we would be doing the Calash's work for them."

"N'Clect* is right!" a thousand thousand thousand voices proclaimed. "Let the one called Forty-seven go forward and do battle with Wall. Let us put our faith in Life."

And there I was, a small slave boy from the Corinthian Plantation, being cheered by a number that added up to a billion. And even though I couldn't count nearly that high I was loved and applauded by them. John leaped on my shoulder and shouted out my name. And then the name Forty-seven was on the lips of the whole hive.

*I didn't know it at the time but N'Clect was John's real Talamish name.

14.

Sunlight glittering through the leaves roused me. I sat up, rubbed the sand out of my eyes, and realized that I was alone. Looking around for my friend I saw that there was a young doe at the edge of the empty space created by the tree. Timidly it looked at me. It was equally afraid and curious and so moved forward and back, keeping its place but at the same time still ready to flee. A mother deer emerged from the bushes then. She cast a wary eye on me and then nuzzled her little fawn. Instantly the young deer calmed down. I could see that there was a berry bush where the two stood. They were eating the sweet fruit and so dared the danger that I represented.

Even though I was afraid of being alone and scared of what Tobias would do when he caught me, I was still enthralled by those deer. I wondered what it would have been like if my mother, Psalma, had lived. Would she have stood over me, protecting me while we ate sweet berries?

While I lamented the loss of my mother Tall John strode

into view. Not the tiny orange and violet John with flames above his head but the colored slave boy with the skinny chest and coppery skin. I wondered then if my dream was real. He stepped in between the mother and child, stroking their flanks and saying something I couldn't hear. They pressed their snouts against him in a friendly way and then went back to eating. John then turned toward me.

In his right hand he carried the napkin that Flore had wrapped my cookies with. He held the big handkerchief by the corners like it was a sack.

"Good morning, Forty-seven," he said upon reaching me. "Did you sleep well?"

"They gonna kill us, Numbah Twelve," I replied.

"Would you like to flee to the north?" he asked.

"I ain't jokin' wit' you, fool."

"I'm not telling a joke," he said. "If you wish we can head north right now. By day after tomorrow we'll be in a place that doesn't have slavery and doesn't return slaves."

"Ain't no sucha place," I said.

"There are many lands that don't have slaves, Forty-seven. Canada, Vermont."

I could tell that he was serious, that he was willing, with no more than a shrug and a nod, to take me away from all the chains and chiggers and cotton. All I had to do was say yes and the misery of my daily existence would have fallen away.

"What you got in that napkin?" I asked him.

"I went back to my bag in the tree and got a chemical that will kill the virus in Eloise's brain. I also collected various fungi that will carry the serum through her blood."

"So if we run away she'll die?"

"Probably."

"But if we wait and run away later can we take Flore and Champ and Mud Albert with us?"

"No," John said. "Only you."

If I ran Miss Eloise would die, and my friends would remain slaves no matter what I did. I couldn't imagine a life where Eloise was dead and where I'd never lay eyes on Big Mama Flore again. The only choice I had was to go back to Corinthian, and I knew that I would at least get bull-whipped for running away.

I could feel the lash on my back even as I stood there in that primal paradise. Fear of the whip brought tears to my eyes. But the thought of leaving my friends and the thought of the Master's daughter dying was too much for me.

That was the way it was for the short while that I knew Tall John from beyond Africa. Everything he said to me was both a test and a lesson. Being his friend was my first experience with the responsibilities of freedom.

"We bettah get back," I said.

"But you said that they would kill us," John argued. "Wouldn't it be better to run?"

"But that girl is dyin'."

"But she's related to people that make Negroes into

slaves. Wouldn't it be better to let her die? Wouldn't it be better for Tobias to feel like you do about the suffering of your people? Anyway, Flore and Mud Albert will be slaves if you go back or not."

I looked up at the strange boy who had befriended me. At first I thought that he was making fun of me. But when I looked into his face I saw that he really expected me to have no feelings for Eloise and even the other slaves.

"No," I said. "I wanna run. An' I sho nuff don' wanna die. But I'd be lonely without my friends in Canaland and I don't blame Miss Eloise for my sufferin'."

"One day you will have to leave the plantation, Forty-seven. Your destiny is far from here."

"Come on," I said. "Let's get back before I change my mind about runnin'."

The sun was out and John was able to move fast again. So it wasn't too very long before we got to the plantation. I wanted to go right out in the fields and start working, pretending that nothing had happened. But John ran us right up to the front porch of the Master's home and knocked on his door.

Fred Chocolate answered. I knew we were in trouble when a worried look came into his sour face. I knew we were dead.

"Run," Fred said. "Run away from here you stupid niggers. Run."

"I've come to see Tobias," John said.

"Tell this soft-headed fool to run from here," Fred said to me.

I grabbed John's arm but his feet were planted like tree roots. There was no moving him.

"Bring Tobias Turner to me," John said in a stern tone.

Fred fell back a step and then a voice came from somewhere in the house.

"Who is that you're talkin' to, Fred Chocolate?" It was Master Tobias.

My guts turned to water and my knees were no sturdier than blades of grass. Tobias came to the door, pushing the butler aside.

"What's this?" he cried. "The runaways. Call Mr. Stewart, Fred. I will have these boys whipped in front of all the slaves out here. Whipped until their backs is bloody and their heads hang down dead."

"No!" Big Mama Flore cried.

I saw her run into the big sitting room behind our enraged Master.

"They just boys, Master Tobias," Fred said.

And even though I was afraid for my life I was amazed that the snooty house Negro would have stood up for two pieces of field trash like us.

"Mr. Stewart!" Tobias cried.

"You can kill us, Tobias Turner," John said in a voice that could not be ignored. "But will you allow us save your daughter's life before you do?"

The russet-hued lad held up his napkin-sack of medicine.

"What are you sayin', Number Twelve?" the Master asked.

"You sent us to find medicine," my friend said proudly. "We've done that. We had to go far away and we got stuck in the rain. I couldn't let the herbs we carried get wet and so we had to hide until the rain stopped."

"The rain quit late last night, nigger!" Mr. Stewart said from behind us.

He had just gained the porch in answer to Tobias's call. I could feel the stamping of his hard boots on the wood beneath our feet. Every time his shod feet hit the planks I imagined him trampling on my bones.

"We fell asleep," John said to Tobias. "We were tired from searching for the medicines your girl needed."

"You can break her fever?" Tobias asked. His voice was lower now. I could hear the sorrow and exhaustion in his words.

"Yes, sir," John said, as serious as a hangman.

"Then come on upstairs before it's too late," Tobias said.

"Number Forty-seven has to come with me," John told Tobias, and I really wished he hadn't. All I wanted to do was to get back out in the cotton fields; back to where I was just a slave and nobody white talked to me or worried about my whereabouts.

"I can't let two filthy niggers in my little girl's room."

"You'd rather let her die?" John asked.

He was no longer acting like a downtrodden slave. Tall

John was talking to Tobias in just the same way he spoke to me. As a matter of fact I believed that everything John was doing and saying was for my benefit. He wasn't worried about the Master or the plantation boss or stuffy Fred Chocolate. He was showing me something. And maybe I would have understood his lesson if I wasn't scared down to the wood beneath my bare feet.

Tobias was shivering with rage at the impudent slave and also in fear for his daughter's life. If John would have listened to me I could have told him that the slave master held a grudge longer than he'd remember any good deed. I could have told John that talking like a white man to a white man was the quickest way for a slave to meet the Lord.

"Come on!" Tobias shouted.

He ran back into the mansion and John followed. I fell back, hoping that I could get away, back to the cotton fields, but Mr. Stewart pushed against my shoulder and I was thrown into the doorway of the big house.

We ran along through the sitting room, with its posh couches and chairs. My dirty bare feet scuttled over the soft carpeting. And even though I was soothed by the feel of the fabric beneath my feet I thought that it was not nearly so elegant as the bed of leaves beneath that great tree where I slept the night before.

We ran up the stairs: Mr. Stewart, Master Tobias, Tall John, Flore, Fred Chocolate, and I. There we came to a big double door that was open. The walls of that room were lined with large windows and everything was covered with yellow lace. The curtains were lace and also the canopy over the bed, even the walls were painted like the creamy material.

Under the canopy, in the center of the room, in the oversized bed, lay the girl-child Eloise. She looked frail and pale with her eyes closed and sounds of distress coming from her lips.

"The fever is taking her brain," John said in an offhanded manner. "She will not live out the morning unless she is treated."

Next to the bed was Eloise's light-skinned maid, Nola. Nola was hardly older than I. She had freckles and greenish eyes and crinkly reddish-brown hair. It was general knowledge among the slaves that Nola was Tobias's daughter by a slave named Patrice who had died some years before.

Nola was crying over her white half-sister's agony. It was plain to see that she loved Eloise as much as I did.

Many slaves loved their masters. Looking back on it now it seems odd — loving someone that keeps you in chains and runs roughshod over your life. But back then the only rule we knew was the white Masters' rule, and so if the Master were ever kind many of us felt grateful because we didn't know any better. And if somebody like Eloise, who never said a harsh word, was somewhere for us to catch a glimpse of now and again, we felt a swelling in our hearts, hoping that such a kind soul would somehow ease our sufferings. That's because the human heart is always filled with hope and the need to love.

So Nola loved Eloise. She would have happily died in her stead.

"Shall I save your daughter, Tobias?" John asked arrogantly.

"Out of the way, Nola," the defeated slave master said.

"No!" Nola shouted.

Mama Flore took the unwilling girl by the shoulders and pulled her away from the dying white girl's bed.

"Come, Forty-seven," John said as he moved toward the girl's side.

Grabbing me by the arm, Tobias said, "Wait a minute. You ain't said what you need this nigger for. He's been on my plantation since he was baby. He don't have no healin' in 'im."

"Where I am from," John replied, rather impatiently, "we cannot heal without teaching. Forty-seven is my student. If I didn't have him I could not save your daughter."

Tobias released me and John unfolded his napkin on the bed.

Even now, over a hundred and seventy years later, in the twenty-first century, I remember the feelings I had in that white girl's bedroom. I was afraid for Eloise because she looked so drawn and deathlike. I was afraid for myself because John had made me part of his haughty procedure. And even while all that fear was in me I was aware that the

Master had lost all of his high-minded ways. He was giving in to a mere slave because that slave might be able to do what they could not. This was possibly the most important lesson John ever taught me; that our so-called masters were not all-powerful, that they were also weak and vulnerable at times. But at the moment I was too frightened to understand the significance of that knowledge.

Upon his open napkin there were various leaves, mushrooms, and twigs. There were also two smaller versions of the soft-glass tubes that he had used to heal my hands and brand. These tubes were so small that they might have been seeds.

John put his hand on Eloise's brow. Nola screamed at him to stop touching her mistress. Flore then dragged the child from the room. John was busy crumbling up the vegetation and mixing it with oil from the capsules he'd gotten from the yellow bag. Then he rubbed the paste up under her upper lip.

"What are you doin' there, Twelve?" Tobias said in a threatening tone.

"Saving your girl if you let me be," he replied.

John crushed another tube and then ran his fingers under the unconscious girl's tongue.

This intimacy was too much for the white man. He grabbed Tall John by the shoulder and threw him nearly across the room. The youth hit the floor with a loud grunt and reached back to rub his head.

I didn't know what to do. John was my friend. I wanted to protect him, but I couldn't stand up to that white man. He could have killed me with just one blow.

Tobias advanced on the prostrate boy. There was death in every gesture of the white man's body.

"Master!" Flore shouted. "Her eyes."

Tobias turned to see his girl looking at him. She held his gaze for a moment and then looked away as if something else had captured her attention. I looked in the direction of her gaze but all I saw was a bare wall.

Tears sprang to my eyes. Eloise was alive and so John and I would be spared. We saved the Master's daughter. He might even grant our freedom. Defeat and death turned around in a flash, like lightning.

"Thank you, Lord," Flore cried.

"She's cured," Tobias said.

"Not yet," John announced. "You threw me off before I could finish the treatment."

"What else do you have to do?" Tobias asked warily.

"I can only show you," said the slave in the voice of a free man.

I could see the two feelings in the slave master's face. He had never had a Negro speak to him thus. For such a slight he was duty-bound to punish the offender. But on the other hand he loved his daughter more than anything. I could see all that in Tobias's visage as plainly as I could see the fingers on my own hand.

Finally Tobias said, "Go on then."

"Come, Forty-seven," he said to me. "This is the hardest part."

Together we went back to the girl's side.

John leaned close to me and whispered, "You have to show her the way back."

Before I could ask him what he meant he took a step back and held out one hand to me while placing the other on the girl's brow.

The moment I took John's hand I was no longer in Eloise's room. Instead I found myself in a field of yellow flowers. I was naked standing next to the girl. She was naked too.

It was broad daylight above us but at the horizon (which seemed to be very far away) night had already fallen. Just at the place where the land touches the sky there hung a beautiful crescent moon. Eloise was staring at that moon. I realized that she had been gazing in that direction even in her bed. Her face was turned fully toward the eerie lunar glow.

She took a step toward the horizon.

I took a closer look at the moon, and in the dark harbor of its arc I saw the grinning skull of Death. I knew then that Eloise had been so close to dying that she had almost completed her journey when Tall John gave her the medicine.

I realized that it was my job to keep her from going toward the darkness under that moon.

But there was a serious problem. I was a black slave while she was the white-skinned daughter of the Master. I wasn't supposed to touch her even with clothes on. I wasn't even supposed to speak in her presence. I was afraid that if she became aware of me she'd scream and her father would slaughter me for molesting his child.

She took another step.

"What should I do, John?" I called out, half hoping that Eloise would hear.

But John didn't answer and Eloise moved another step toward the darkness.

The horizon seemed much closer now. Eloise was no more than a dozen paces from her death.

"Miss Eloise," I said softly.

She made no sign that she heard.

She took another step.

"Miss Eloise," I said boldly.

But still she didn't hear.

"Miss Eloise!"

She took two steps, moving faster now.

She was beginning to run toward the night.

I knew then that there was nothing else I could do. I ran after her and grabbed her by her pale shoulders. She struggled against me but I used all of the strength in my young limbs to drag her back toward the sunlit field of yellow flowers.

"Let me aloose," she cried.

But I didn't stop until we were in the light again, until there was no darkness or crescent moon anywhere to be seen.

Still she gazed toward the place where the skull-face of

Death had loomed, but I stood in front of her, blocking her line of vision.

She noticed me and then looked down at the flowers around her feet.

When her gaze came back to me she asked, "You're one of pap's niggers ain't you, boy?" she asked me. "The one that was spyin' on me from the barn."

She didn't seem concerned about our lack of clothes. Actually she didn't even seem to notice.

"Neither master nor nigger be," I said fearfully. I had to say it but I felt that even though the sky was clear I'd be struck down by a bolt from the white man's God.

"Where are we?" Eloise asked.

"You sick, miss," I said. "Me'n my friend Number Twelve is tryin' to make you bettah. You was walkin' in a deathly direction but I grabbed you an' dragged you back."

"Are you usin' slave magic?" she asked.

"I reckon we is," I said. "It sho seem like it."

"I hear Nola cryin'," Eloise said, cocking her ear.

I could hear it too. The soft sobs were coming from nowhere it seemed.

"Back in yo bedroom ma'am," I said. "She's back there worried that you about to expire."

"But I won't die?"

"I don't think so. Not today anyway."

"So you saved my life," she said, staring into my eyes.

"I s'pose so. You were strayin' toward Death an' we brung you back home."

"What's your name?" she asked.

"Forty-seven."

"Thank you, Forty-seven. Thank you for savin' my life."

I appreciated her gratitude but there was something else that was even more important to me. I really *had* saved her life. I had used my mind and my courage to brave Death and Master Tobias to do what I thought was right. These actions made me a man, and a real man, I knew, could never be a slave.

From that moment on I never thought of myself as a slave again.

Suddenly I was back in Eloise's bedroom. She was awake and staring into my eyes. She smiled and I knew that she was going to live.

"Is she gonna live, Number Twelve?" Tobias asked in a loud voice.

"Yes, sir, I believe she is."

"All right then. Mr. Stewart?"

"Yes, boss?"

"Take these two filthy niggers and throw them in the Tomb."

I felt rough hands grab me by the shoulders. Two white men ran in and knocked John to the floor.

John had a look of terror and shock on his face.

"What are you doing, Tobias Turner?" he asked with a crack in his voice.

"What I should'a done the minute you stood up an'

called me by my name," Tobias said. "This is no house of abolitionists. You will pay for your crimes."

"But I saved your daughter," John said. I could hear the pain and confusion in his words.

"God saved my child," Tobias said. "And now I shall do his will by punishing you."

One of the white men hit John in the face and he fell unconscious.

"Check his pockets to see what else he stole from me," Tobias told them.

The only thing they found was the cigar-shaped sleep inducing device. Tobias took that and put it in his pocket. Then the white men dragged John from the room.

I was deeply shocked by this brutality. After all, I had just come from a bright field of beauty and saving the Master's child. But those men didn't care how I felt. The men who held me battered me around the shoulders and head and dragged me from the room.

Flore yelled out, "babychile!" and I called out for her, but to no avail.

15.

The Tomb was a tiny shack that had once been an out-house. It sat in the middle of the yard and Mr. Stewart used it to punish slaves without permanently damaging them. It was no bigger than a deep coffin on the inside with just enough room for a male slave — or two smaller boy slaves, as we found out.

Mr. Stewart chained us hand and foot and tied us together. Then he locked the door behind us. It was dark in there and filled with biting maggots and ticks. As the sun bore down on the yard the heat rose in there until it was hotter than I had ever known.

"Are you all right, Forty-seven?"

"No," I answered petulantly. "Here I am in the jail when I should be free all'acause you had to go talkin' to that white man like he was a babychile."

"But we saved his daughter," John said in the darkness, where I was sure we'd die.

"But you a niggah, man," I cried. "An' ain't no niggah

gonna ever speak to a white man wit'out givin' him his proper due."

"Neither master nor nigger be," he said in the darkness.

I wanted to strangle those words out of his throat but I knew that he was just ignorant of our ways. It had been less than a day since we had shared the dream of his land with his tiny, rainbow-colored people. But a lot had happened since then. Part of me thought that his land of Elle on the ocean named Universe was just a dream. But I knew in my heart that it wasn't, that Tall John was really from beyond Africa and had to be forgiven for not knowing that he was inferior to the slave master's power.

"Listen, Forty-seven," John said. "That's the reason I need you. I've lived among your people for many years but I've never understood their brutality. I was always on the outside — passing through."

"But you been a slave," I argued.

"I always had the power to shrug off my chains and escape. I never really paid all that much attention to the people I met along the way because I was looking for you. I suppose that I always looked down on everyone I met and therefore never realized how they felt. Not until now when all of my power has been drained off to save the girl Eloise."

"That's why you need me?" I asked. "To understand how slaves feel?"

"No. Wall is coming."

"That's Mr. Pike?"

"Yes. He is a great power among his people. Much greater than I. You know how to survive against forces much greater than you. You are the teacher and I am the dunce. Without you there can be no future for anyone."

And even there, in my greatest danger, I felt the urgency in John's words.

"Deep under the ground in your world there is a kind of metal," John continued. "It looks like green powder but when it is spun at a great speed it starts spinning on its own and goes even faster. It picks up speed more and more until finally it goes so fast that it tears apart the glue that holds the universe in place."

"And Andrew Pike want that green powder?"

"Yes. He wants to make it spin and blow up everything."

"Why would somebody wanna do sumpin' like that?"

"Because," John said, "in another place beyond the world where we see and breathe there is a river of consciousness —"

"That's what you said before. But what do the countesses river got to do with green powder?"

"Not countess but consciousness — psi — what thoughts and dreams are made of," John explained. "You and I and all of my people and all of yours —"

"You mean Champ and Mama Flore too?" I asked.

"And Tobias and Eloise," John added.

I didn't say anything but I was surprised that John saw Tobias and me as belonging to the same people — as if we were the same race. This set off a way of thinking that was more alien to me than anything I had experienced up until that point.

"So all of us are here but at the same time our idees an' our dreams is swimmin' in this river?" I asked.

"Exactly. It is in a place beyond space and time. It is another place that cannot be touched or seen or heard."

"Except if'n you spin that green powder," I added.

"No, but that's what Wall believes," John said in the dark.

"An' this Wall is also Andrew Pike?" I asked.

"Yes. His people, after they split off from our race, developed a taste for the small trace of spirit that makes its way into our bodies. They suck out the energy and souls of sentient beings for their sustenance. But they're greedy; they yearn to obtain the Upper Level where they can feast on the God-Mind."

"So all this man Pike, who really is Wall, gotta do is dig down an' git that green powder an' then everything gets blowed up?" I asked, trying to string together all he'd said.

"No," John said. "First he must acquire a machine. When Wall got here he sent off a message telling his people to send this machine from a colony they have in this galaxy. When it arrives it will be able to mine and then spin the green powder. Wall and the Calash believe that this will open the universe to their perverse appetites."

"How long before it gets here?"

"One hundred and eighty-seven years."

"We all be dead by then," I said, thinking that John and I would probably be dead before the next day dawned.

"Maybe so," John said, "and maybe not. But regardless there is another quicker way that he might attain the green powder."

"What's that?" I asked.

Listening to his story I forgot my situation. I was more worried about that green powder than I was about the bugs biting me and the heat sweating me to death.

"I came here in an extremely powerful craft called the Sun Ship," he said. "The engine of that ship can be altered to help Wall excavate the green powder. Wall must not have it."

"And you took this ship on the Universe Ocean to come here?"

"Yes."

I didn't even understand most of the words he said. But I could feel the urgency in his tone. I could feel his fear. And even though I was in dire trouble myself I worried about my friend and my world.

We stayed in that hotbox all day. After a few hours I began to swoon in and out of consciousness.

"I think I'd like to go up north now," I said to John once when I had awakened.

"I can't take us for a while," he said. "My power was greatly weakened by the healing of Eloise. I won't be able to flee or even unlock these chains for a day or two."

What could I say? He'd only saved Eloise because I had asked him to. It was my fault just as much as his that we were in the Tomb.

While we wasted away in the hot stench of our prison I worked my wrists around in the manacles. My sweat made the skin so slick that I was finally able to slip free.

"John."

No answer.

"John."

A slight moan sounded from where my friend lay in the pitch black of our prison closet.

"John, I got my hands free," I said. "Maybe you could too. Maybe we could get outta here an' run."

"Too . . . weak . . . ," he whispered. "Too . . . hot . . ."

"But you gotta try," I pleaded. "If we don' get free an' run mastuh gonna kill us."

"No master . . . ," he choked, and could not finish the admonition.

I reached out and touched his shoulder. I could tell that he was slumped backward, hanging down in his chains. This was the first time I had been with Tall John that he was helpless. I realized then that he was a person just like I was, that he could suffer and need help too.

This was yet another major moment in my young life. There I was in chains and still I was worried for my friend. I was trying to get free so that I could steal us both away from Tobias.

That's what running away for a slave was — theft. Because taking myself from the plantation meant that I was taking the master's property — me — away from him.

Somewhere in my mind I realized that it was absurd to think that a person could steal himself. But I also knew that if I told a white man these thoughts I would be put instantly to death, so I couldn't share my rebellious ideas with other slaves.

Deep in my mind an even more radical thought had begun to form. I realized that I was free even though I was clamped in chains and locked away. I was free because I had made the decision to run away if I could. Most of the slaves on the Corinthian Plantation would never actually try to run away. They knew that they'd probably get caught and whipped or worse. And I could see that the real chains that the slave wore were the color of his skin and the defeat in his mind. *Neither master nor nigger be,* Tall John had said from the first moments we met. There in the worst aspect of my slavery I came to fully understand those words' meaning.

I felt the thrill of freedom in my heart.

"John," I said. "John, I understand. I know what you been sayin'. I ain't got no mastuh 'cause I ain't no slave."

He sighed in the darkness but made no words that I could understand. John's weakness set off a great trepidation in my heart. I believed that only he could understand the freedom that I had just come to realize. Without him I would be as lost as he was on the ocean called Universe.

"John, how can I help you?"

"Touch . . ."

"What?"

"Touch my head . . . with your hands," he said.

I reached out and felt around until I could feel the pulse in his temples. One beat, two beats, three beats, four . . . and then there came a bright yellow light that filled our foul cell. I could see John sagging down in his chains with his eyes closed and his breath coming fast and short like the panting of a winded dog.

Then I was gone from the tomb and free from my bonds. John and I were sitting side by side in crudely built rocking chairs out in front of a small, ramshackle cabin that stood on a rise looking down over a pine forest. There were larks singing and fat clouds floating in the blue sky overhead. John was there next to me.

At first I thought that I had swooned and fallen into a dream.

"No," Tall John from beyond Africa said, answering my thought. "You are not dreaming. We are here together — in our minds."

"Where are we?" I asked John.

"I don't know. Don't you recognize this place?"

Suddenly I realized that we were in front of Britisher Bill's place; a cabin that Una Turner's father had given to the slave, Britisher Bill, when he earned his freedom. I used to go there with Big Mama Flore and Mud Albert when I was very small. Master Tobias would send us with a basket of food that the old master had promised to deliver to Britisher Bill every fourth Sunday for the rest of his life.

Flore and Albert would walk hand in hand and every once in a while they'd stop and Flore would kiss Albert's cheek. Once they sat on a log and hugged for such a long time that I got bored and asked them when we were going to leave.

"How did you know about Britisher Bill's cabin?" I asked John.

"I didn't," he said, "the memory is in your mind."

Britisher Bill appeared in my mind then. He was older than Mud Albert by far and he spoke in an accent that people said was English. The old master had gone to Jamaica long ago and purchased Bill for his personal manservant. He became so fond of the slave that he brought him back to the Corinthian.

"But," I said, shaking the image of Bill from my mind, "if you too weak t'work your magic then how did we get here?"

"The power is in your mind, Forty-seven. Your mind brought us here. I merely showed you the way."

"So can my mind bring us water an' food?" I asked. "'Cause you know I sho am hungry an' thirsty too."

John leaned back in his rocker and sighed.

"You could imagine eating chicken," he said, and somewhere I heard the cackle of a hen, "but when we go back to our chains you will be all the more hungry."

"So we ain't got aloose from the Tomb?" I asked. "We just daydreamin'?"

"Don't you like it better here than in that hot cell?"

I looked around at the peaceful yard and the forest beyond and thought, *Yes, this is better than chains.*

"Back there," John said. "I'm almost dead. I wouldn't be able to give you my last words, my council."

"You not gonna die, John," I protested, but in my heart I feared his words were true.

"I should have listened to you, Forty-seven," he said. "I am well over three thousand years old and so I thought a boy of fourteen couldn't tell me anything. I was so sure that I could master Tobias just as he had mastered you. My pride was my downfall and now I have put the entire universe in jeopardy."

"You cain't be worried 'bout no universe when we in trouble right now in the Tomb," I scolded.

"Right again, Forty-seven. I can feel my mind fading. I must tell you what you need to know before I pass on to the Upper Level. Listen closely.

"I had intended to give you guidance and power with which you could fight against Wall and keep him from his mad plan. Now it's too late for that. I will die in Tobias's chains but you may yet survive. If you do I want you to find my yellow bag and study its contents. Certain items therein will speak to you —"

"Things gonna talk to me like them oil seeds you use for healin'?"

"You will see something," John said patiently, nodding slightly as if he were tired and soon to fall asleep. "And after a while you will have a nagging feeling at the back of your mind. And soon you will know how to go about using that thing."

I noticed that the sun was setting. This was odd because when we first came to Britisher Bill's cabin, only a few minutes before, it was high noon.

"Time is running out for me," Tall John sighed. "I was arrogant. I didn't listen to our hero."

"You not gonna die, John," I whined. "We gonna both make it through this. You just tired, that's all. You just sleepy. If Tobias meant to kill us he'da send us to Mr. Stewart's killin' shack. All you gotta do is sleep an' build up yo' strength. Tomorrow he'll prob'ly send us back to the slave quarters. You'll see."

I helped John out of the rocking chair and laid him out on the ground.

He smiled at me and said, "So you forgive me for delivering you into Tobias's hands?"

"Ain't nuthin' to forgive," I said. "It was me wanted t'come back. It's my fault we here."

Hearing this John smiled and then fell into a deep sleep. As he closed his eyes the sun set on Britisher Bill's cabin. In the darkness the pine forest and the sky faded, becoming the close walls of our cell. The scent of pine was replaced by the odor of human suffering. As the darkness descended I realized that our cell might be an actual tomb for both of us.

* * *

When the night came the heat didn't let up and even the little light that had filtered in with the sun was gone. I came awake, lamenting my sad fate. There I was chained by my ankles with no water or food, dying. And what had I done wrong? I had helped to save the master's daughter. I had come back home even though it meant a life of slavery.

"Numbah Twelve?" came a voice from outside of our hotbox.

"Eighty-four?" I answered.

"Is Johnny in there wit'you, Forty-seven?" she asked through the door.

"Yeah but he out. It's 'cause'a no watah I think."

"I brought you an' him some watah an' two apples," she said. "Mud Albert sneaked out an' unchained me an' give me this here from Flore."

And with that the food slot opened. I could feel the cool breeze of night coming in through there. She handed through a small water skin and two apples. Because my hands were free I was able to reach out and take her gifts.

"Tell him that I be prayin' for you. I sure will."

The girl that John called Tweenie closed the food slot and I held the jug to his lips. At the first taste of the water on his tongue he made a sound in his throat and roused. I held the cup to his lips until he drank every drop.

When he realized that he'd finished the water he asked, "Did you drink already?"

"Yeah," I lied. I figured that he needed the water more

than I did and, anyway, the fruit that Eighty-four gave us had water in it too.

We each ate an apple. I devoured mine, core and all.

This is another moment that I have to stop and explain the crazy contradiction of the pain of slavery. Those apples certainly weren't the best that I've ever eaten. I have traveled, in my many years, near and far across America and beyond. I have eaten the most delicious fruits that our rich soil has to offer. But that mealy little apple that Eighty-four fed us in our prison was the sweetest, most delicious thing that I've ever tasted. No great meal of succulent pork and sweet potatoes could ever be so satisfying. That's because we were starving. We were near death. And those small spotted fruit contained the taste of salvation.

In the morning the door to our cell was opened and we were dragged out into the light of day. All around the yard stood the field slaves, in chains. The house slaves were also there — Fred Chocolate, Big Mama Flore, Nola, and the rest of the servants. Sitting on fences and wagons all around were Mr. Stewart and a dozen or so white riflemen. Dead center of the yard was a huge wagon wheel leaned up against a hay wagon.

When I saw that big wheel my heart went cold.

John and I were thrown to the ground and Master Turner came out wearing a black suit like Andrew Pike had worn the day he interrupted Ned's funeral.

"We are here today," Tobias said, "to punish the disrespect, thievery, and mutiny of these two niggers, Number Twelve and Number Forty-seven. They are bein' punished for talkin' back, for stealin' a handkerchief, and for runnin' away while on business for their master. I have brought out all you other slaves so that you will see and learn, so that you will remember not to forget your place in the scheme of things as God has decreed.

"I have to punish these boys because it's the responsibility of the white man to keep the black from forgettin' his place. But I am not unfeelin'. I could have both of you boys whipped until you were dead. But I know that po' Forty-seven was led astray by this new nigger here. So the punishment for Number Twelve is twenty-four lashes and a visit to Mr. Stewart's shack . . ."

"No!" Eighty-four shouted. I saw her try to run out into the yard but her chains and the women around her held her back.

"And as for Forty-seven, he is to receive just twelve lashes —"

Mama Flore ran out into the yard yelling words that made no sense to me. She was tearing at her breast and running right for Tobias. A big white man stood forward and knocked Flore down with the butt of his rifle. The moment he did that Mud Albert ran out. The rifleman swiveled and shot Albert in the chest.

All of this was almost too much for me to take in and so when Champ Noland also broke line and was beaten to the ground by other white men I hardly noticed. All I could see was Mama Flore like a lump on the ground and Mud Albert crawling toward her and bleeding like a well-pump bringing up water.

Albert made it almost to Flore's side but then he stopped moving. I'm sure that was the moment of his death.

"Get on with it!" Tobias Turner shouted then.

John was dragged to the wagon wheel and chained to it hand and foot. Mr. Stewart counted out the lashes as a big white man named Thaddeus Murphy worked his bullwhip in a hideous way.

John didn't cry or shout. He just took the lashes and hung down. When that was over they put me in his place.

I cried and shouted for Mama Flore. I begged and screamed and finally I passed out. Before I lost consciousness I had a vision of myself as a young child sitting on Flore's lap and playing with her ears.

"You got big ears, Mama Flore," I remembered saying.

"You got little bitty ones," she said, "like chocolate seashells."

And then I passed out.

16.

My back was on fire when I came awake in the slave cabin that afternoon.

"You niggahs really messed up," Pritchard said.

I couldn't see the lame carpenter but I knew that he was standing there behind me.

"Yessiree," Pritchard cackled, "you niggers just had to act all uppity and now you see what you get. Mud Albert dead, Champ Noland in the Tomb. They say that Mama Flore is in her closet gettin' ready for her harp."

"Mama Flore dyin'?" I cried. "Naw it ain't true."

"You see?" Pritchard said. He came into view on my left side, leaning on his crutch and grinning. "You see? Talkin' back to your betters is why you got them sores on yo back. That's why Numbah Twelve out in Mr. Stewart's killin' shack right now. That's why Mud Albert is dead in the barn."

My heart was devastated. Mud Albert dead, Mama Flore dying. Champ Noland, the most powerful man anyone had even seen, chained and beaten. All of that happened because I asked John to save Eloise. And even though he had saved the girl and even though I was happy that she was alive, I was miserable at the cost of her survival. Everyone I had ever loved was destroyed.

I was in terrible pain but still I lifted myself from the slave cot. I wasn't surprised that my feet weren't chained. The wounds on my back were so bad that they probably expected me to die. The bullwhip does dreadful damage to human skin. It tears all the way down to bone. I was bleeding from a dozen crisscrossed tears in my flesh, but still I got to my feet at the foot of the bed.

"Are you crazy, niggah?" Pritchard cried. "Git back in that bed before somebody white sees you."

"Get away from me, Pritchard," I said. "I'm small and I'm hurtin' but I will find a way to get back at you if you get in my way."

"It ain't me you got to worry 'bout, boy. It's Tobias an' Stewart and every white man from here to the border of Tennessee that's gonna be after you."

I made my way to the cabin door. Every step I took I worried about falling down. But I kept on walking because of the hatred in my heart. I had never felt like that before. Tobias had taken everything from me, everything except John and I would die before I let Mr. Stewart destroy him.

I had never been to the killin' shack before but I knew where the path was that led there. I stumbled out behind the slave cabin and then down the trail that had been the doom of so many black souls. There were birds crying at my passage but to my wounded heart they sounded like the tormented voices of all of the slaves Mr. Stewart had tortured and killed.

I didn't know what I would do when I got to my destination. I probably wouldn't live out the day but I didn't care. My friend needed me and I would not let him down.

I lumbered through the vegetation, feeling the raw wounds on my back with every step. When I looked down I could see the blood trickling to my feet. But that didn't stop me. I just took one step after another down the evil lane.

After some time I came to an open yard. Across from where I stood was a dilapidated cabin. I knew that was where I'd find Mr. Stewart and Tall John. I reached down and picked up a throwing rock that had sharp corners on two sides. I took one step and then someone grabbed me by my arm. I turned to hit that someone with my rock but before I could swing I saw that it was Eighty-four standing there in her worn blue dress.

"What you doin' heah, Forty-seven?" she cried, pulling me from the road.

"I came for John."

"Me too," she said.

"That's the killin' shack," I said.

"I s'pose it is," Eighty-four agreed. "Mr. Stewart is in there right now killin' my baby."

"I guess we got to go in there if'n we wanna save him," I said.

"Yeah," she said.

But neither one of us moved. Faced with the certain death of the killing shack we were frozen. Our entire lives we had been trained to fear Mr. Stewart. Our entire lives we were told that the white overboss had complete power over us. Our fear was like an invisible wall standing in the middle of that yard.

Eighty-four reached out a finger and touched my cheek. "You cryin'," she said.

It was her touch that pushed me past the line of our fear.

"You git a big stick," I said. "Git a big stick and then we gonna go up that porch. I'ma go in an' th'ow my rock an' when he chasin' me out the do' you try an' hit 'im on the head."

Eighty-four nodded and looked around for a stick. She found a tree branch that was as big as a club. That was the first time I looked at her as something other than chattel. She was a young woman and beautiful as Tall John had said. She was stronger than many men I knew and the love in her heart for John found a companion in me.

We strode toward the door of the cabin. Eighty-four moved to the side and I pushed the door wide.

When I got into the room I took in everything at once. The first thing that assailed me was the smell. It was as if Mr. Stewart had stored rotted meat in the walls. It stank and burned my eyes. There was a long table in the middle of the floor and John was stretched out across it. The leather bands lashed to his wrists and ankles were attached to heavy baskets that had cannon balls in them for weight. My friend wasn't screaming but I could see the pain in his face.

Mr. Stewart was standing over the table with his back to me. When I hefted my stone I realized that my strength was waning. I had only one chance to hit Stewart and then run. I doubted that I would have been able to make it across the yard.

I threw the stone. But even as the missile left my hand Stewart must have sensed my presence, because he turned as the rock flew through the air. Everything worked together and my rock met his left eye. Stewart grabbed at his head and then fell to the floor.

I staggered to my friend's side. On a shelf next to the table was a knife. I used this to cut the bonds that held John's hands. I expected the basket connected to his wrists to fall but I was surprised when he was dragged down to the other end of the table. Then I realized that the heavy basket tied to his feet no longer had the counterbalance of the other basket and it pulled my friend to the other end.

John sat up and grabbed his ribcage.

"It hurts," he moaned. "It hurts. So this is what it means to suffer."

"Can you git up?" I asked him.

"Pain," he replied.

I used the knife to cut the bonds around his ankles and then I helped him to the side of the table. He tried to get to his feet but his legs gave out like they were rubber. I got down on my knees to help him but just as I did a shadow fell over us.

"I'll kill botha you niggahs!" Mr. Stewart shouted.

He was there above us, blood coming from his ruined eye.

Before I could do anything he was on me. I felt his hands close around my throat.

"Damn you!" I shouted, thinking that at least I could condemn his evil soul to hell before he killed me.

"Huh!" he exclaimed, and his grip loosened.

I thought that maybe my curse had instant effect. Stewart fell to the side and there above me stood Eighty-four, the club clutched in her hands. She dropped the log and helped both me and John to our feet.

"Take me to my yellow sack," he whispered in my ear as we went through the door.

John could hardly walk and I was weak from the bleeding wounds on my back. Without Eighty-four we would never have made it. She nearly carried John and I supported myself by holding onto her shoulder.

After a long time we came upon the tree where John kept his shiny yellow sack. He opened it up and took out a little red lacquer box. From this he brought out a metal disk that stood upon a spindly tripod. He did something with the legs, and the disk started turning slowly. Then he collapsed.

"We'll be safe for a while," he whispered. "Have to sleep."

He fell unconscious and soon after I followed.

In my dreams I was being chased by a one-eyed monster who was at once one of the Calash and the wounded Mr. Stewart.

17.

"Wake up, boy," someone said. "Wake up."

In my dream I was floating on a square raft down a wide river. The sun was glittering in my eyes and warming my skin with its bright rays. A great she-bear stood on her back legs at the shore and roared me welcome.

"Wake up, boy," a female voice said. She shook me gently but still the wounds on my back felt as if hot coals had been dropped on them.

"Ow!" I cried.

I opened my eyes to see Eighty-four sitting there in the glow of something like lamplight. It was a steady orange radiance emanating from the tripod that John had set up before he passed out. After a moment I realized that it must have been nighttime because out beyond the orange glow was darkness.

"You crazy, Eighty-four? We cain't have no light in the night. They'll see us out here."

"He said no," she whispered. "He said that they cain't see us 'cause'a his little lantern."

She didn't have to say who *he* was. I knew that John had set up some magic to protect us.

"He bettah?" I asked.

"Not hardly," Eighty-four said. "He crawled off an' said that he had to do sumpin' to make his legs an' arms not be so stretched out. I said that I'd help him but he bade me to stay here wit' you."

I figured that he was probably going to do something so strange that he thought he might scare Eighty-four. Maybe he was going to turn back into a tiny little orange and purple man, I thought. And then I wondered about that. How could I have gotten so far away from a slave's everyday life that I was thinking about magic and defying the white men that owned me? That wasn't me. I bowed my head when white men addressed me. I said *yassuh* and *nawsuh* whenever they asked me a question. How did I find myself in the night, half dead, thinking about magic and so deep in trouble that nothing I knew of could save my life.

"I love him," Eighty-four said.

"You do?"

"Uh-huh. He was so sweet to me them days that we picked cotton. He talked to me like he could see right in my heart. An' I know he felt sumpin' fo' me too."

"He said, 'that Eighty-four's a beautiful girl,'" I added.

"He said that?" She seemed amazed.

"Yes, ma'am. He said that you were just as pretty as Miss Eloise. And I do believe he's right."

Eighty-four grinned and leaned over to kiss my brow.

"You a nice boy," she said. "I sorry I was so mean to you that day we pick cotton."

"Shoot," I said. "Pickin' that cotton make a mad dawg out of a bunny rabbit."

Eighty-four grinned some more and touched my cheek with her calloused palm.

"Maybe Numbah Twelve and you and me can get away somewhere where they ain't got no slaves," she said. "Maybe him an' me get married and we could raise you as our boy."

Even though I was weak and hurting I felt something grand about her including me in her dream. All John had to do was give her a few nice words and she changed from a sullen bully into a woman filled with hope.

"How are you, Forty-seven?" John asked then.

We both turned and saw him emerge into the orange light. He was walking upright and full of strength. It was as if all of Mr. Stewart's tortures had amounted to naught. John winked at me and I knew that he had done some powerful magic.

"Was you listenin' to us?" Eighty-four asked warily.

"Only a little bit, Tweenie. I was happy to see you and I didn't want to interrupt."

The slave-girl bowed her head. I knew that she was embarrassed at what she had said. I think she was more worried about him knowing what she felt than she was about the white men that had to be after us.

Just as I had this thought I heard the braying of Tobias's

hounds. There was a yip and then a loud howl. And we all three knew that the white men were hunting us down.

"Put out that light, Numbah Twelve," I said.

"No one can see us as long as this light shines," he replied calmly. "They can't see us while we remain within the light of this disk."

I had no idea of what his words meant. And even though I trusted him I knew that he was capable of making mistakes. After all, him thinking that saving Tobias's daughter would keep the plantation master from hurting us is what got my friends beaten and killed.

The hounds were getting closer. I could hear each one barking and calling for black blood.

"We got to get outta here, baby," Eighty-four said to her man.

"Forty-seven is too weak," he answered. "And if we move away from my little machine the dogs will run us down."

"They'll smell his blood if we stay here," she argued.

"No," he said. "You have to trust me, Tweenie. I know what I'm doing."

"You didn't know so good when you got yo butt tied up in Mr. Stewart's shack," she said.

"If you run Tobias and his dogs will tear you to shreds," he said. "But if you stay, and I survive, we will be married in a church and Forty-seven here will grow into a man who will save the whole world."

"If we run we can do that."

"If we run Forty-seven will die and the world will pass away with him," John said.

Eighty-four gazed at me with an emotion in her face that I could not decipher. Maybe she hated me for standing in the way of her happiness. Maybe she wondered at the deep connection between me and her man. I had no answers for her. John and his war with the being called Wall was just as much a mystery to me as was the sun in the sky or the secret to how birds learned to fly. All I knew for sure was that he was right about my wounds. I couldn't have risen to my feet if an angel flew down and bade me to follow him to the Pearly Gates.

Just at that moment a dog bayed not ten yards from where we sat. Eighty-four and I turned our heads to see, at the furthest extreme of orange light, the snout and tail of one of Tobias's hounds! The dog was tinted orange by John's glowing apparatus. It seemed to glance at us, or at least in our direction, but then he turned away, howled, and ran off into the night.

For a moment I saw one of Tobias's men come into the glow but he just looked through us and then went on after the dogs.

We all sat silently for long moments after the hunters had gone. The dogs' braying faded into the distance.

I was so tired that when I closed my eyes I couldn't open them again. But I wasn't quite asleep. I could still hear John and Eighty-four talking.

"What we gonna do if'n we cain't run?" she asked.

"When the sun comes up," he said, "I can take you and Forty-seven one at a time to a special place."

"An' we just gonna wait till then?" she asked.

"I guess."

"Then why don't you come ovah here an' sit next to me t'keep me warm?"

I heard a rustling and then I passed over into the darkness of sleep.

18.

When I awoke I was laying face up upon a large flat stone. The sun was hovering above the level of the pine trees. I could see its red glow beyond my feet. The pain from the whipping wasn't as bad as it had been before but I was still very weak. Even the morning sun couldn't warm my bones or brighten my eyes.

"Forty-seven," John said.

"Yeah, John?"

"I'm sorry but you are dying."

"I am?" I could hear Eighty-four crying but I couldn't see her.

"I'm sorry," John said. He was standing to my right, looking down on my demise.

"It wasn't yo fault," I said. "I was the one wanted to go back and save Eloise. I'm glad we did it but I feel terrible about Mud Albert. If I die will you bury me next to that river we saw? The one where the bears was."

"You won't die," John said. "At least not today."

"But you said —"

"I said I was sorry. I wanted to wait a while before we became brothers. I wanted you to grow into a man and learn the heritage of your race. A young man like you will find it hard to wage the kind of war that is bound to arise between you and Wall and his agents."

"His agents? Like sheriffs?"

"Something like you will be for me," John said.

And even though I was dying I got exasperated by his riddles.

"What you tryin' t'say, nig —" I stopped myself from using the insult and my friend smiled.

"I am going to perform a ritual that my people have been doing since before any man walked on the earth," he said. "I am going to put my cha into yours. You will still be you but you will begin to know everything I know and everything my people have known. You will have power that no human being has ever dreamed of. And with that knowledge and that power you will save the world."

It was as if I were in a dream. I saw John in that morning light even though darkness seemed to be descending. I heard his words, but they might have just as well been a memory.

John nodded and Eighty-four came into view. She sat next to me on the big stone and took hold of my shoulders. And then John sat on the other side of me. The light of morning seemed to gather around his head and his visage became saintly like the pictures in Tobias's illustrated Bible that Big Mama Flore used to sneak and show me.

John brought his hands behind his neck and grabbed hold of the light. He lifted it up above his head. It looked something like one of the Calash though not hard and angry but gentle. The appendages wrapped themselves around John's fingers in a friendly caress. Then my friend placed the living light upon my chest. The insubstantial tentacles released him and wrapped themselves around my body and my head. I felt a sense of joy so intensely that I couldn't remain still.

"Hold him down, Tweenie," John commanded.

Eighty-four tightened her grip.

He grabbed hold of me too.

I didn't want to fight them but as the creature of light pressed itself into my heart and mind I pushed hard to free myself. I kicked and screamed and bit and shouted. I twisted and knocked my head against the stone below me. As the light filled me I had the desire to fly, to rise above the world and see the oceans and the continents. Continents? How did I know about continents? I wondered. How did I know the names of oceans and constellations and phrases in languages both human and inhuman?

I screamed and threw Eighty-four and John off of me. I rose to my feet and raised my hands to the heavens. All around me were lights of every hue, many that have no names in any human tongue. A billion billion little rainbow people tittered in a place far away and long ago and even far into the future.

And then everything went black.

* * *

"Forty-seven," Tall John from beyond Africa said in a booming voice.

I was lying on the ground next to the stone bed where I had lain. I was naked and confused. I wanted to rise but there were so many thoughts going through my head that I couldn't manage to get my legs working.

"Ain't I dead?" were the first words out of my mouth.

In the back of my head I could hear the chatter of a thousand beings. I didn't understand what they were saying but I was sure that they were talking to me.

"In a way you are," John said. "Your body will no longer age, no longer will it experience the processes of a normal human being. From now on you will be the age you were when we met."

"What did you do to him?" Eighty-four asked. There was wonderment in her eyes but no fear. I realized that her love for him somehow expected his power. It was no surprise to me that her passion was even more powerful than his light.

"I gave him my cha, or the child of my cha. The infant that will grow to be a full soul within Forty-seven."

"I don't know what you mean," I said. I managed to stand.

I felt different when I stood next to Eighty-four. After a moment I realized that the difference was that I was looking at her eye to eye. I had grown more than a foot. I had trouble standing because my legs were so much longer that I didn't know how to move them.

"The essence of everything I was given to fight Wall has been planted inside your heart and mind," John was saying. "One day you will know everything that I know. You can use that knowledge in your war against the Calash."

"When will that be?"

"So many years from now that everyone you know will be long dead."

The idea that all of my friends would be dead saddened me.

"Even you?" I asked.

John looked away at the sky and Eighty-four put her arm on my shoulder and said, "You growed."

"His body has caught up to his years," John told her. "Flore kept him away from meat and milk so that he would stay small and Tobias wouldn't send him into the cotton fields. My cha has brought him to his full physical potential — and beyond."

The chattering in the back of my mind was subsiding. The pain of my lashes was gone. I reached around but could find no sores or even scars on my back.

"So I'll never grow any older than I am right now?" I asked.

"That's right."

I was happy that I would never have to grow old and sad like the men and women I had known among the slaves. I didn't know what I'd be missing. I'm still not all that sure.

"We got to go save Champ and Big Mama," I said then.

"Are you crazy, niggah?" Eighty-four said to me.

"Not nigger but man," my mouth said the words but I wondered where the elocution came from. Then I wondered about the word *elocution*. I knew that it meant the way words were said but I didn't know how I knew that. All I knew for sure was that the word *nigger* felt like my enemy; an enemy that would grind me into dust and let me blow away on the breeze if I didn't oppose it.

"Champ and Flore stood up for us," I said to John. "Mud Albert gave his life tryin' to help Mama Flore. If I didn't he'p'em then how could I do anything else worthwhile?"

The words came from me and the feelings did too. But I could feel the little creature of light in amongst them. It was as if the hero that I always wanted to be in my heart was set free by my friend and now I would never be a nigger again.

I went down a small path to a pond and looked at my reflection in the water. I was taller but not so tall as a full-grown man. My body had filled out some too but I was still of a slight build. And on my shoulder was stitched the Number 47. The scar of slavery would never be gone from me. And as long as I lived that memory would be alive.

19.

We waited until nightfall before John and I made our way back to the Corinthian Plantation. We left Eighty-four behind because John was going to use a second sound machine he'd found in his yellow bag and that would put her to sleep along with the rest of the plantation. He didn't tell her that, though. He said that two could move around better than three. She didn't argue. I think that Eighty-four had made up her mind never to step foot on the master's estate again.

It was nigh on midnight when we entered upon the main yard in front of Tobias's mansion. John walked onto the porch with impunity but I was more timid. Even though I had seen his machine put everyone to sleep before I was still nervous that if a sound could put someone to sleep then maybe another sound could wake them up. And if I made that sound then they would awake to see me sneaking around the white man's rooms.

I was scared to death but still I had to see Big Mama Flore.

Flore had been the center of my life and she stood up to protect me when my twelve lashes were announced. She was mother to me and I would have done anything to save her life.

I went to the closet where she slept but there was another woman there. It was Clemmie, Mr. Turner's old nursemaid, sleeping in Big Mama's place.

"Is she dead?" I asked my friend. "Did she die while you were savin' my life?"

John put his hands on top of his head and shut his eyes tight. It was like he was trying to *remember* where Flore had gone. He stayed like that for a minute or more. And while he was thinking I felt something like a pinch at the back of my neck. It was so sharp that I rubbed my hand back there but there was nothing I could feel. I understood somehow that I was feeling John's mature light searching around for Flore. I knew that some day I would be able to do the same thing.

John opened his eyes and said, "She's in the barn."

I was running as soon as the words were out of his mouth.

I found Flore on a pitiful mattress of hay. Her face was drawn and ashen. The bruise of where she was bludgeoned loomed large above her brow.

She was asleep, as was everyone, but her breathing was shallow and weak.

"Is she dyin'?" I whined.

"If we don't do something soon she will die," John said.

While he spoke I saw something on the hay behind him.

I went into the corner and beheld the most heartbreaking thing I had ever seen.

It was the body of Mud Albert. He'd been stripped naked and the blood had been washed from his wounds. He lay upon the burlap sack they would bury him in. His eyes were still open and his beard hairs seemed brittle and sparse. One hand was across his chest but the other was up to his shoulder curled into a claw-like hook.

I remembered all of the kind words and wise words Albert had spoken to me over the many seasons of my slavery. Looking down on him I realized that he died because of his love for Flore. It came to me then that no one should have to die for love.

"She must have a vascular cleansing to hasten her recuperative powers," John said as he threw a blanket over Mud Albert's small frame.

He often spoke in big words like that but this was the first time I understood what he was saying. It struck me as odd but I didn't have much time to think about it because I was mourning Mud Albert.

"What can I do?" I asked.

"If we put her in a wagon and took her to where my sack is I might be able to relieve her symptoms some. She has had a serious trauma to the head so she might be a little slower."

"Steal a wagon from Master Tobias?" I was worried about my adopted mother but stealing from a white man was certain death in Georgia at that time.

"We can leave her," John suggested.

I was enraged by his offhanded manner. It was as if he didn't care if Flore lived or died.

"Don't be angry with me, Forty-seven," John said. "What you're worried about is true. It will be hard to keep out of sight if we have to carry Flore. And if we're all captured she will die anyway. Sometimes we have to make hard choices."

It was a tough call. Here the woman who had raised me was near death and I had to brave death in order to ease her pain.

"Let's do it," I said, full of fears and trepidation.

"You go on and find Tobias's carriage," John said. "I'll stay here and get her ready."

I went through the barn door into the yard. The carriage was kept next to the vegetable garden so I went off looking for the mule Lacto that had crippled Pritchard.

The mule was nowhere to be seen but when I came to the rear of the mansion I saw Tobias's buggy still hitched to his great gray mare. The mare was just standing there with her back leg crooked so I knew she was asleep. Gently I roused her by rubbing between her eyes and then I led the sleepy horse and buggy back toward the barn.

As I was crossing the yard someone shouted, in a raspy dry voice, "Hey you, boy."

Coming toward me was a white man with a pronounced limp. As he shambled closer I was able to make out various details about his features. His head was bald, that was the first thing I noticed. After that I made out the eye patch. A shiver went through me and I was so frightened I didn't even think about running.

Closer still I could see that the skin all about the top of the man's head had been sewn like leather.

"Stay right there," the man said, and I knew it was Mr. Stewart.

"You dead," I said.

"Hallelujah and I am risen," he replied, a big smile crossing his ugly maw.

In his right hand I could see the bullwhip. And even though I was healed I could feel the pain of my twelve lashes all over again. He raised his arm and released the lash but before it could reach me — before I could even think — I was a quarter of the way across the yard looking at Mr. Stewart from the side. After the bullwhip cracked in the air he turned and smiled.

"You lookin' a little taller, Numbah Forty-seven," he said. "Look like you gotta new master too."

Again he swung at me and again I moved faster than I could think.

"Neither master nor nigger be," I said, standing at a spot eight feet from where Stewart's bullwhip bit.

"Fool," he said, and then snapped his whip again.

Six times he swung at me and six times I avoided the whip. On each swing the lash got closer. The last time I felt the breeze caused by its passage.

But I was ready to run again. What I hoped was that John would hear us and come out. I didn't want to call to him because then Mr. Stewart would have known that I had an ally. If I kept my friend's presence a secret I hoped that we could overcome him by stealth if not by strength of arm.

There I was in the year 1832. There was no electricity yet or flying machines or laser beams; the glorious miracles of the twentieth century had not been invented and so when I looked upon the walking corpse of Mr. Stewart I could only think of magic, evil magic. Somehow a spell had been evoked and Stewart had become a zombie. He was the walking dead and everybody knew that a walking dead man could only be put back in the grave by the use of salt or silver — and I didn't possess either one.

The onetime overboss was maybe twelve feet away from me but I was prepared to defend myself. Somehow I had gained the speed of a wildcat. I knew that there was no man in Georgia who could catch me. I waited for him to draw back his whip but he surprised me and jumped!

He hurtled through the air even faster than I could run. I made it four steps and he came down, catching me in the crook of his right arm.

Everything that happened next came to pass in a few seconds but those few seconds felt like many long minutes.

As Stewart's arm curled around my waist I stepped up on it and over his grasp. I skipped a step away but before I could run he caught hold of my ankle. I turned around then and pushed on his hand, moving my foot before he could get a solid hold. We were face to face for a moment. I could see that his skin color was paler than it had been and he smelled wild, like a dog after he's rolled around in something foul. I had no time to consider those things because the one-eyed man pushed me and as I fell he rose up, intent upon falling on me.

I made it into a crouch but I have never in my very long life been in a tighter spot. If I turned to run the human Cyclops would jump and take me down. If I stayed there all he had to do was reach out and seize me.

In that standoff, which lasted no more than two seconds, I noticed that Mr. Stewart's eye-patch was made from wrought iron. All across, the metal was etched with delicate designs. In spite of my situation I wondered, *Where could he get such a thing?*

Mr. Stewart bent down a bit and I knew he was about to jump. I prepared to avoid his lunge but my chances, I knew, were no better than even.

The slave boss grinned.

"Begone!" The word boomed all around us.

I was amazed by the splendor of that voice but Mr. Stewart grabbed his head and fell to his knees. When he went down I could see John a few paces behind him. He was standing tall and regally.

"Begone!" he intoned again, and Stewart raised up on all fours and scampered away like a cur running from a lion.

"Quickly," John said to me then. "We must be away from here."

"What about Mama Flore?" I cried.

"There is no time," he said. "Big trouble will be here soon."

20.

The next thing I knew we were running through the woods, moving quickly between the boughs and branches. My feet were sure and swift and I didn't have to rely on holding onto my friend.

After we had had run for some time I stopped. When he realized that I was no longer following him John stopped too.

"Come on," he said. "We have to get away from here before he comes."

"You already chased Mr. Stewart away," I argued.

"Not the ghoul but his master," John said.

"Who?"

"The one you know as Andrew Pike."

I remembered the tall man on the chestnut mare who had interrupted poor Ned's funeral. For some reason it set off a thrilling in my heart. But I refused to give in to fear.

"Why would he be coming after the Corinthian?" I asked. "I thought he was only after you and that green powder."

"He is," John said. "He thinks we're on the plantation. He'll go there first. In the meantime we can get away. You don't know enough yet to protect yourself from his power."

"But what will he do to the peoples on the plantation?"

"I don't know," John said. "But I'm sure that he will come in force."

"But what about Mama Flore and Champ and all the other slaves?"

"All we can do is hope that they survive the attack," the strange bronze-colored boy said, hanging his head down.

"Attack? What attack?"

"It's like I told you before. Pike wants something that I have — my machine. It has the power to dig into the earth and excavate the green powder. With that he could start a chain reaction that would disrupt the entire universe. He would kill every being on this planet to obtain my machine. So you see I can't go back and help the others."

Something about the light that John put into my chest allowed me to understand his words. I understood the word *planet* and what that entailed. I could almost see all the species of life throughout the world: trillions of hearts and minds from the lowliest insect to the great sperm whale.

"But every life is holy," I said, somehow knowing this was the truth. "And without Mama Flore I'm sure I would have died a long time ago. If she had let me die I would never be able to help you and your people."

"We can't go back," John said.

"We have to," I countered.

When our eyes met I understood the relationship between the disguised alien and me. He had seen stars up close and the infinite variety of the place he called Universe. I had seen suffering and hard-won survival for every moment of my brief existence. And, while he knew much more than I did, I had a deeper knowledge of what it meant to be on the brink of losing everything. That's why he needed me, because I would make the choice for living against any odds.

I think these same thoughts went through Tall John's mind because he bowed his head again.

"You are the chosen hero," he said. "I must follow."

And even though I wanted him to say that he would go with me to try and help my slave family I had to wonder why he would do so.

"What do you mean — chosen?" I asked. "How was I chosen and who in hell chose me?"

"The answer, like your true name, Forty-seven, is in your blood. You and a few others like you have the perfect blood code to hold the powers of the Tamal. And you, unlike many others, have a pure heart and an innocent view of the world. Even the fact that you would go back to your friends after almost being killed by Wall's ghoul proves that you have a brave soul and true spirit."

"What happened to Mr. Stewart?" I asked then.

"He died in the human way under the log that Tweenie swung. But Wall in the guise of Andrew Pike must have come upon him before the vitality had gone out of his blood. Wall resurrected him to do his bidding."

"If he can do all that then why can't he build his own machine to dig down in the ground for that powder?"

"The Calash are not as evolved in technology as are the Tamal," John said. "They work mainly with biology. They even travel through space using certain unique qualities of their anatomy. Wall needs my machine or it will be more than a century before he will receive the power to try again."

"So it's our job to keep Wall from getting to your machine?" I asked.

"Yes."

"I promise to help you do that if you help me save Mama Flore and Champ and as many slaves as we can."

"As I said," John replied, "I will follow your lead."

When we got back upon the Corinthian Plantation it was just before dawn. Everything was calm.

"Are they still under your spell?" I asked John.

"No. Everyone is sleeping normally. But look." John put his hand on my shoulder and pointed to the woods on the other side of Tobias's mansion. Somehow his touch allowed me to see what he could with his superior alien perceptions. Suddenly I could see behind the woods, making out a group of a dozen or so heavily armed men. The one-eyed ghoul, Mr. Stewart, was in their lead.

All of the men were white, armed with rifles, and had pistols and knives shoved into their belts. They were moving stealthily toward the big house and the workmen's dormitory.

"Quick," John said. "Hurry down and release as many slaves as you can while I warn Tobias and his men."

Before I could run he added, "I will be weak from the effort of waking the slave master's clan, Forty-seven. You will have to save your friends alone."

Maybe if I had time to think about his last words I would have changed my mind. But I was mostly thinking about saving my friends.

"Where I find you aftah?" I asked John.

"Under the hanging tree," he said ominously.

I nodded and then I was gone.

I ran as fast as I could toward the Tomb, having made up my mind that Champ Noland was the first man that I had to free.

Again I was amazed at how fast I could run. I moved as nimbly as an African cheetah and so was in front of the small prison in no time at all. But when I got there I saw that it was padlocked.

I knew where the key to the Tomb was kept because of all the years I'd spent near Mama Flore. It was on a hook in the kitchen. With my newfound speed I ran to the back kitchen door. I found a ring of keys hanging from the hook. Then I hurried toward the Tomb and tried three keys before one of them opened the padlock.

"Champ!" I cried.

He was curled up on the floor with his head down between his knees. When he heard my voice he roused himself and raised his eyes to see who had opened his door.

At once I went to work finding the right key for his manacles.

His face was all bruised and the flesh above both his eyes was swollen from beatings. There was dried blood about his mouth and there was something wrong with his jaw.

"What you doin' here, Forty-seven?"

"Men wit' guns comin'," I said, still fumbling for the right key. "We gotta get the other slaves and run 'fore they kill us all."

I might have been John's people's hero but Champ Noland was mine. He took in my words and forgot his pain and torture. I found the right key and his chains fell away. He rose up and strode out of that prison just as if it was any other door. He knew that if Tobias had seen him defy his punishment that he would be killed no matter how valuable he was as a worker and a stud. But having heard my call he rose to the task regardless of the danger.

"AWAKEN, TOBIAS TURNER AND TENNESSEE BOB AND WILLIAM THORNDEN AND MILLER JONES!" the voice boomed in my head so loudly that I lowered almost to the ground.

"What's the mattah, Forty-seven?" Champ asked. "You shot?"

"Don't you hear it, Champ?" I said.

He pulled me to my feet and started dragging me toward the slave quarters.

"RISE ALL YOU MEN OF THE CORINTHIAN PLANTATION!" the voice boomed again. "BRIGANDS ARE ATTACKING WITH MUSKETS AND KNIVES!"

I knew that it was John somehow speaking in my mind and in the minds of all the sleeping white inhabitants of the Corinthian Plantation. I could hear the voice because of the light in my chest but Tall John wasn't speaking to the slaves, and so Champ remained ignorant of the call.

As we moved toward the slave quarters the voice got weaker. And by the time we were at the men's cabin I could barely make it out at all.

"Wake up, boys, they tryin' to kill us all!" Champ yelled as we barged into the men's quarters.

"What you doin' here, Champ Noland?" Pritchard asked as he rose up from Mud Albert's mattress.

I realized in that instant that Pritchard had been given the job as the new top boy in the cabin. Mud Albert wasn't even in his grave yet and the cowardly, mean-hearted Pritchard had already taken his place.

Champ stepped forward and struck Pritchard a mighty blow while still shouting, "Wake up, men, they comin' to kill us!"

Champ took the key from Pritchard's belt and ran from cot to cot unlocking shackles.

"Go to the women's cabin," Champ told Number Thirty-three. "Run down there and tell 'em all to run!"

Thirty-three, a tall slave with coal-black skin, hesitated for just a moment, then he grabbed the keys from Champ's hand and ran out the door. Meanwhile all the men I had sweated and strained with in the cotton fields leaped from their cots. The sun was coming up and I heard a crack from over where the mansion stood. After a moment there were more cracking sounds and someone cried, "Gunfire!"

The men started shouting then. They rushed out of the cabin and scattered. I came to the door and in the first weak rays of dawn I could see fighting in front of the master's mansion. There were flames rising from his house.

"Mama Flore!" I shouted, and then I was running.

21.

White men were firing their muskets and fighting hand to hand in front of the mansion. I saw Tobias and two of his men struggling with the bald and disfigured Mr. Stewart. Stewart had superhuman strength. As soon as one of those men jumped on him he'd throw that man off as if he were a child. Tobias and his men kept coming though.

It was a terrible sight but I didn't have the time to worry about what happened to Tobias and his people. All I cared about was Mama Flore.

The flames from the mansion had spread to the barn. I hastened to Mama Flore's side. She was still unconscious. I tried to lift her but the speed John had given me had little effect on my strength. I could barely lift one of Mama Flore's big arms.

I could hear the yells and struggles outside of the barn while the flames crackled around, closing in.

"Wake up, Big Mama!" I cried. "Wake up! It's a fire!"

When she didn't stir I took her by the arm, intent on

dragging her from the blazing barn. I had managed to move her about three feet when my strength gave out.

I looked around to see if there was a blanket that I could roll her onto. I thought maybe pulling the blanket under her would allow me to move her. In one stall I saw a blanket and grabbed it before realizing that it was the pall John had used to cover Mud Albert's body. I was mesmerized by the uncomfortable pose of his death. I thought that he would remain like that through all eternity, all twisted up and suffering because of Tobias and his evil.

I hurried back to Flore's unconscious body.

I was afraid of being burned to death in the barn but I couldn't bring myself to leave the only mother I ever knew. I begged her to wake up but she was still unconscious from that white man hitting her.

The barn door was just beginning to burn when it burst open and Champ Noland came running in. He went to Big Mama and took her up in his arms.

"Come on, boy," Champ told me. "Let's go out the back and put Flore in the carriage."

Even though the back door was covered in flame Champ managed to kick it open.

I saw that he'd found the carriage that I'd led to the barn earlier. He hefted Flore into the back, jumped up in the driver's seat, and turned to help me up, but I was already at his side using my newfound speed.

Champ yelled at the gray mare and we took off. There

was gunfire now and then and plenty of shouting from the fight in front of the plantation. On our way down the road behind the mansion a white man, Roger Brice, jumped at us.

He landed on the side of the buggy and yelled at Champ, "Pull this wagon ovah, niggah!"

For the first time in his life Champ did not obey the direct order of a white man. Instead he lifted Brice by the front of his pants and threw him off into a ditch on the side of the road. The bearded white man hit the ground hard and he didn't rise to continue his attack.

Champ and I looked at each other then, and even though we didn't say a word we knew the content of each others' minds. Champ had used his great strength to fight back against a white man. He might have killed that man. It wasn't just a crime punishable by torture and death but it was also unheard of in the history of us slaves. It was as if he had broken some higher law that would call down hellfire upon us.

I had already conspired to attack Mr. Stewart with Eighty-four. I had thrown my rock at him. Eighty-four had struck him in the head. But neither act seemed as bad as a full-grown man-slave going against a white man. A man-slave throwing off the yoke of slavery meant that the rules we had lived by our entire lives had been broken.

We both turned our heads to the sky, looking for God's retribution. But it didn't come. Champ yelled at Tobias's horse again and we were hurrying away from the scene of the battle.

*   *   *

In the distance we could see the tall flames rise from the Corinthian Plantation. The sounds of the battle faded but then I heard something like both a gasp and a scream.

"Did you hear that, Champ?" I asked.

"What?"

I heard another scream. It was a girl.

"That," I said.

"I don't heah nuthin', Forty-seven," Champ replied, cocking his ear.

"Stop the wagon, Champ. Stop it."

He did as I said just as soon as he was sure that we were hidden behind a stand of dark trees.

"What's wrong, boy?"

"You know where the hangin' oak is?" I asked him.

"I guess I do," he said. "They hanged the man I called uncle from there onceit."

"Numbah Twelve will be theah waitin' for me. You go to him and I'll be by in just a while."

"Where you goin'?"

"Hand me that rope from under yo' seat," I said.

Big Champ Noland did as I asked and I ran off in the woods faster than a deer fleeing a cougar.

Running through the deep forest toward the sound of the girl's scream, I realized that it wasn't one girl yelling, but two.

I was agitated and afraid for my life and the lives of the only family I had ever known. But even though I was so distressed it was still amazing to me how I managed to run through those woods. My feet moved surely between the low-slung branches, and if there was no place to stand I easily climbed high and moved quickly through the upper branches like a wily chipmunk avoiding some land-bound predator. At times I was nearly at the top of the trees, finding the fastest footholds there.

I was at such a lofty place when I saw Mr. Stewart fall upon Eloise Turner and her faithful servant, and half-sister, Nola. Eloise, dressed in a mere slip and barefoot, was trying to evade the leather-skinned madman while Nola, wearing only a nightshirt herself, was standing to the side yelling for help.

Stewart grabbed Eloise and lifted her in the air.

"Help me!" she cried, and I remembered when Pritchard had slapped me silly and branded me.

I knew I had to save those two girls. I knew I had to face my fear of the man who daunted me since as far back as I could remember. But before I could steel myself Nola ran forward and threw a rock, hitting Stewart in the head. That blow would have knocked any ordinary man out cold. But Elias Ainsworthy Stewart was no longer an ordinary man. He had risen after Eighty-four delivered a fatal blow to his head, and so Nola's pebble wasn't going to bother him.

The stone made a metallic sound upon striking his skull, and for a moment Stewart froze, tilting his head as if he had forgotten something. Eloise was screaming and I chose that moment to jump down from the tree.

I came down on the ground behind Stewart. I made to run up to him but I tripped on something soft. I was up on my feet soon enough but then I saw that the obstacle that made me fall was the body of Tobias Turner. He was lying half on his side with his head turned at an impossible angle. He wore black pants and a white shirt with the tails out and no shoes. It was his bare feet that made me feel sorry for him. The big difference between the master and all of his slaves was that he was always shod and we never were. Now that he was fallen down to our level even the musket lying next to his outstretched hand was impotent.

I stared at the man who I'd always thought of as master, until the coming of Tall John. I felt sorry for his death, angry at his life, and glad that he could never hurt another slave. These feelings struggled against each other in my heart. A slave has a thousand feelings about his slaver. This is because that man has the power of life and death over his slaves and even though you might be hating him you also pray that he will show you mercy.

I might have sat there all night between those emotions if Nola hadn't screamed again.

"You leave my mistress be, Elias Stewart!" she shouted, and then she screamed like a banshee.

Quickly I tied a loop in the rope I got from the carriage. I tied the other end to a poplar sapling. Then I came up behind the living ghoul — Mr. Stewart. When he raised a foot I put the loop about his ankle and pulled hard. The one-eyed goliath fell and I lashed his feet together.

chapter twenty-one

"Damn you, boy," Stewart bellowed.

He released Eloise in order to grab at me but I was too swift. I ran all the way around him, seized Eloise by the wrist with one hand and Nola with my other. We all three took off through the woods.

As we ran away Stewart roared an evil curse.

Eloise was so frightened that she stopped running.

"Come on," I hissed. "We gots to go."

"Yeah, Miss Eloise," Nola echoed. "We gots to get away from that man."

"I'm scared," she cried.

"We all scared, babychile," I said. "Scared is the lamp that lights the way."

"Yes, suh," Nola said.

They were words that Flore had often said to me. They had the right effect. Eloise pulled her tattered slip around her and hurried with me and her light-skinned servant through the dark wood. The three of us moved quickly amid the howls of Mr. Stewart's rage.

22.

It didn't take us long to come to the hanging oak. Because we could make a straight line through the woods while Champ had to take a longer road we all arrived at the same time.

There were alarm bells ringing throughout the valley by then. People on other plantations had seen the fire and smoke rising from Corinthian and so they were coming to help out. The hanging oak wasn't on any direct path and so we knew that we were pretty safe.

Tall John hadn't shown up yet but I wasn't worried about him. I had the feeling that if he were harmed I would have felt it in the light in my chest.

"What you doin' wit' her here, Forty-seven?" Champ asked me when he caught sight of Eloise.

"Mr. Stewart was tryin' t'kill her and Nola," I said. "I took 'em away from him."

"Take me home," Eloise cried.

"No, Miss Eloise," Nola said. "That Mr. Stewart's still out there. An' he must be untied by now."

"That's yo home, girl," I added, pointing at the smoke rising with the sun. "It ain't safe for you there yet."

Eloise looked at the thick black plume and took a deep breath. "My father will stop that traitor," she announced. "And he will give all you slaves a chicken dinner and set you free for bein' faithful and savin' my life."

At one time that would have been my only dream, to be given freedom by my master. But *neither nigger nor master be* had become a reality for me. And even though by Georgia law I was now the property of Miss Eloise Turner I expected to take my own freedom — come what may.

"Yo' daddy's dead, girl," I said.

"No," Eloise replied sounding almost reasonable. "Mr. Stewart hit him but my daddy only fell down senseless."

"No ma'am," I said. "He fell down all right but his neck broke when he went down. I saw him."

"No!" Eloise protested.

She looked around at Nola and the slave girl wrapped her beloved mistress and half-sister in her arms.

Champ pulled the buggy behind the hanging tree and I climbed in the back to see how Flore was doing.

Her skin had gone dull and her eyes were open but it didn't seem like she saw anything. I called her name but she didn't answer. When I stroked her cheek I felt that she was burning hot.

"Forty-seven," Tall John from beyond Africa said.

When I turned around I saw that my friend had retrieved

his yellow sack. As John approached us from the deep wood Champ faltered and then fell to the ground. He clutched at his foot, the foot he used to kick open the burning door.

Quick as anything John brought out a tube of healing wax and slathered it on Champ's bloody burns. He then climbed into the wagon and began to examine Flore.

The sun was coming up and there were the sounds of dogs braying all around.

"Let's get these people into the woods," John said.

He took a tarp from the back of the buggy and laid it on the ground. Then he and I together pulled Flore from the carriage and lay her on the thick blanket. Then we pulled with all our might, dragging Flore into the forest.

"Come on, girl, and help us," John said to Nola.

For a moment she gave her mistress a worried look but then she ran to our side and helped haul the unconscious slave behind the trees that stood witness for so many years to the hangings of so many slaves and criminals.

"Is she gonna live?" I asked John when we were hidden.

"I think she might if you didn't bring every white man in the county down on our heads."

"Don't you worry about that, Numbah Twelve," I said proudly. "You just leave that to me."

With that I ran out to the buggy, grabbed the reins, and yelled, "He-ah!" The mare threw back her head and ran out into the road.

Champ yelled but he couldn't stop me because of his

burned foot. John called for me to stop but I ignored his command.

I didn't use the buggy whip on the horse. Somehow she and I both knew that she was supposed to run. The buggy raced down the road, bumping over ruts and stones. We were headed for the main road that crossed the path to the Corinthian Plantation.

We, the gray mare and I, had made it about a mile when we heard a yell.

"Hey, you, nigger!"

I turned my head to see a group of about five white men on foot surrounded by half a dozen hounds. Behind them came two white men on horseback.

"Run, horse!" I yelled, and the beast understood. She whinnied and then kicked her feet as if it were the devil himself on our trail.

The horsemen came after us. And no matter how fast my horse could run she was still hindered by the weight of the buggy. We were racing down a path between two hay fields. The horsemen were bearing down on us and there was no avoiding them. I could hear their grunts and curses urging their horses to go even faster.

Up ahead there was a wood of knotty pine.

One horseman had made it to the back of my carriage. He leaped from his horse onto the buckboard.

"I'm'onna cut your throat, nigger," he yelled.

I turned my head to see him. He was about to jump on me but we hit a stone and he was knocked off balance.

When he fell I could see that the other horseman was almost upon us.

The man who was in the buggy was trying to get his balance, all the time cursing at me. But before he could make good his threats we reached the edge of the piney wood.

"Stop, girl!" I yelled to the horse.

When she slowed down things around us happened very quickly. First the horse that was pursuing us veered to the right, throwing his rider from the saddle and onto the hard road. The man who was in the buggy was also thrown down. I stood up from the rider's seat and jumped onto a large branch above my head. Then I made it through the trees as if I were a bird playing among the branches.

From the cover of the foliage I could see the five men on foot come up to their fallen friends.

The man who had jumped in the back of the carriage said, "Niggah jumped up in that tree."

Another man, breathing hard from his run, said, "Must be headed north toward the Lippman place and the river."

Two other men agreed with his guess.

I smiled to myself, knowing that I had sent our pursuers on a wild goose chase. I moved into the deeper wood and then headed back toward the hanging oak.

The sun was just now peeking above the horizon.

When I got there Flore was sitting upright and talking with Champ. The pain that had been in Champ's face was gone. Tall John and Eloise were sitting under a tree. He was telling her something and she was listening closely.

chapter twenty-two

Nola approached me.

"I wanna thank you, Numbah Forty-seven," she said.

Hearing these words I longed for a real name. I wanted Nola to know me as person and friend — not a number.

"That's okay," I said, made shy by her steady gaze.

"You seem different," she said. "Like you biggah or sumpin'."

"With all this stuff goin' on," I said, "I think I did grow some."

"When you fought Mr. Stewart that was the most brave thing I ever seed," she said. "Just a boy standin' up to that one-eyed monster of a man. I'll never forget seein' that for all the rest of my life."

She reached out and touched my face and I felt that everything I had gone through was worth it. I *had* saved her life. I *was* a hero, at least on that one smoky morning.

"Where did you go, Forty-seven?" Tall John asked as he approached us.

"I got them white mens to chase me," I said. "And then I run off into the woods where they couldn't catch me or see me to shoot at. They think that we on t'other side'a the valley so they ain't gonna come around heah no time soon."

"What about the dogs, boy?" Champ Noland asked. "What about them bloodhounds?"

I looked around and saw that Tall John had put up his little plate-thing that made the orange light and so I knew we were hidden from even the hounds.

"They won't smell us, Champ. You can count on that."

"I seen them dogs hunt down a man in the rain," Champ said. "We gots to run, Forty-seven."

"You can't run with that foot, Champ," John said. "Here, drink this water and relax."

John handed Champ a small stone cup filled with clear liquid and the hero drank it down. Not more than five minutes had passed when the big man sat down and then laid down to sleep. Eloise was already asleep under the tree where she and John had been speaking.

Only Flore and Nola were still awake. Flore was sitting up on her tarp with her legs stretched out in front of her and with her hands behind her, propping her up.

"Come here, boy," she said to me. "Come talk to yo Big Mama."

I was so happy to hear Flore call to me that I ran to her side.

"How you feelin', Big Mama?" I cried.

"I feel good, baby. But what happened? Where are we? I remembah that Tobias said that he was gonna beat you and then somebody hit me."

I put my arms around Flore's head and squeezed her. I kissed her face.

"Why you cryin', babychile?" she asked. "Is we dead?"

"Naw, Big Mama. We free."

Flore's eyes opened big as moons. She looked at me and then at the tree branches above her head.

"Free?"

The truth was dawning on both of us. We were free.

Free to do what we wanted to do. Freedom — what every slave dreamed about from morning to night and from night to morning, every day of their lives.

Flore's mouth opened and tears flooded her eyes.

"Free?" she said again.

She rocked forward and put her arms around me. When she hugged me I was her little boy again. I grabbed on tight.

In the distance dogs were howling and the smell of smoke was in the air but we didn't care about all of that. We were free under the pale blue morning skies. Even if they caught us and hung us from the tree we hid behind we still had the greatest treasure in the world.

23.

After a while Flore fell asleep too. Nola had taken a sip of Tall John's water earlier on and so she was dozing peacefully.

"Will they find us?" I asked my friend.

"I don't think so," he said. But his brow was furrowed and his words were heavy.

"What's wrong?" I asked.

"There's a place about ten miles north of here where my machine lies hidden under the ground. There's an alarm set on it designed to tell me if one of the Calash is somewhere nearby."

"Did that alarm ring?" I asked.

John nodded.

"Maybe it's just some animal rubbed up against it," I suggested, wanting to calm my friend down.

"No. It's Wall. He has found my ship while I was distracted here with you and your friends. He will soon be able to utilize the mechanism and dig the green powder from the earth."

"Then we bettah go an' stop 'im 'fore he can do that," I said, speaking right up. "You helped me save my friends an' now I'll help you."

John smiled then.

"You would help me even though you are just now free?" he asked.

"If'n we can put Flore an' Champ ovah wit' Eighty-four then I'd be happy that they was free an' you'n me could go an' take that green powder gin away from Andy Pike."

"It will take him a while to open the door," John said. "And together we might be a match for him."

I smiled and shook my friend's hand.

"We gonna do it," I said.

Then John said something that I didn't understand at the time but it struck me as being rather odd.

"Your courage gives me the strength to surrender myself," he said. "All life flows toward the Upper Level."

After that John gave me a drink of his sleeping water and I drifted off into a dream that was not a dream at all.

I was floating in the air among thousands of the tiny, multi-colored people of John's race. Then I felt something pulling and pushing at me, and the sky disappeared and there was nothing above but blackness and stars. I was thrown out of the company of the little people and I was flying faster than anything toward one of the glittering stars.

All of a sudden I knew that I wasn't dreaming about me

but about Tall John when he got into his Sun Ship and headed off toward Earth.

The star I was heading for became as big as the sun. It was a wide field of fire that sang with power and majesty, but I wasn't afraid. I slipped through the white flames of the star and came to a place that was pure and red. It was hot but there was a place right in the middle of the star that was black and cold. I/John dove into the center of the blackness and suddenly I/John was somewhere else. I/John was far, far away from my home, and lonely. I/John would never be home again. All of my people were far behind me while I/John would find star after star traveling so far away from my home that it would be as if there was no home for me, anywhere.

I woke up crying for that loneliness. And I knew somehow that the dream was not really a dream but a lesson about my friend Tall John from beyond the stars. His light was a part of me now and it was telling me about my friend, his history, and my mission.

"You awake, boy?" Champ Noland asked.

It was nighttime. Champ and Flore and Tall John and Nola stood around me as I lay on the ground. The moon illuminated my friends.

"Where's Eloise?" I asked.

"We sent her home," John said.

"She was like in a spell," Nola added. "John put the evil eye on her."

I could see that the newly freed slave girl was of two minds about my friend and his powers.

"Yes," John said. "I put her in a trance and suggested that she tell her friends that we saved her and then headed west for the river. That should give us enough time."

I got to my feet and clasped hands with Champ. Then I kissed Mama Flore and touched Nola's arm.

"Are you still willing to help me?" John asked.

"Yes, sir," I said.

Champ was walking just fine and Flore stood on her own two feet with no assistance. I was happy that Nola was with us. I didn't know her very well because even though she was a fellow slave, she'd been in the service of Eloise and so I had hardly ever crossed her path.

I guess I must have been looking at Nola while having these thoughts because she came up to me then.

"Do you trust that boy they call John, Forty-seven?" she asked softly so that no one else could hear.

"Sure, Nola. He's the on'y reason that we got away alive."

"But before he got here nuthin' ever happened that we had to get away from," she said, looking at me with wide, trusting eyes.

I realized that I was like a savior to her because I had saved her life — her and her mistress Eloise.

"Do you miss Eloise?" I asked then.

"Miss Eloise?" she asked, repeating the last part of my question. "I s'pose that I will miss her. But I can see how things will never be the same. An' even though I love her in my heart I'd be afraid evah to sleep in that house again 'cause I might awake to gunshots and fire."

"You were brave out there, fighting Mr. Stewart to save Eloise," I said. "You're a hero too."

Hearing this made Nola's brow furrow.

"But I was scared to death fightin' that man," she said.

"Me too," I added. "Bein' brave, I figger, is just the othah side'a the coin from bein' scared. If whatevah you fightin' ain't bad enough to scare ya then they ain't no reason to be brave."

Nola smiled at me then and touched my arm. I knew that from that day on we would be the best of friends.

"It's time to go, Forty-seven," Tall John said.

And so we were off through the deep woods that surrounded the cotton plantations.

John was in the lead, holding up an orange light to show us the way.

"Is that niggah crazy?" Champ asked me along the way. "Holdin' up that light so them white mens can find us."

"We free now, Champ," I remember saying. "There ain't no more masters or niggahs or slaves for us. Just free men and free women no mattah what color they is."

"But what about that light?" he asked.

"Only we can see it, Champ," I said.

I didn't know how I knew that but I knew it was true.

When Flore said that she was hungry John gave us all little squares of food that looked like bread but tasted sweet like cake. After eating a couple of those squares I wasn't hungry at all.

We walked for hours before reaching the field where John saved me with his light. Eighty-four was there waiting for us. She ran up to John and kissed him on the lips and hugged him to her. She was happy to see the rest of us too but Tall John was the only one she had eyes for.

The sun was coming up again and John told everyone that we needed to sleep before making it out of the south. He gave everyone a drink of the special water that he carried in his yellow bag, but only Champ and Flore and Eighty-four and Nola went to sleep.

"What now?" I asked my brother in light.

"Now we go after Wall and his minion — Mr. Stewart," John said, hefting his yellow sack over his shoulder.

"Sounds good by me," I said, even though I was quaking inside.

With that John and I took off through the woods while my friends and fellow ex-slaves slept in the clearing next to the big flat stone.

I expected John to hurry us along toward Andrew Pike and Mr. Stewart. But instead he set a slow pace through the woods. There were larks and whip-poor-wills singing in the trees. A dry breeze was blowing and bright sunbeams peeked down through the dark covering of leaves and pine needles. We walked along a shallow creek bed that burbled over large white stones.

For quite a while John was silent on our country stroll. I didn't want to interrupt his reverie. I could tell by the look on his face that he was worried.

I didn't want to know about his fears. The battle at the Corinthian Plantation had been the worst thing that I had ever seen, and from what I understood Andrew Pike meant to cause a conflagration that was on an infinitely grander scale. I didn't care to know about it, fearing that my courage might fail if I did.

After a long time — an hour or more — the smile came back into Tall John's face.

"You must wonder why," he said.

I knew what he meant. It was almost as if I knew what he was thinking. The light he had saved me with had brought us closer than brothers.

"Yeah," I said. "Why me? There's a many millions of peoples in this world. You could'a picked any one'a thems to help you. Heck, you could'a raised a whole army with the tricks you could pull."

"Yes," Tall John said, shaking his head sadly. "And then Wall would raise an army and the whole world would go to war. And war would only benefit my enemy."

"It'a on'y hep him if he win," I said.

"No, my friend. If Wall could start a big enough war he would spur the growth of technology. Man always starts inventing when he wants to win a battle. Soon enough he wouldn't need my Sun Ship to mine the green ore.

chapter twenty-three

Mankind itself would furnish him with the tools he needs."

"But why me?" I asked again. "Why am I here wit' you? Why not a real hero like Champ Noland or somebody at least knows his numbers like Mud Albert?"

Tall John stopped walking and put his hand on my shoulder. When he did this I realized that I had still been growing. I was now taller than he.

"On my homeworld," he said, "we had a machine made of glass. There were a trillion trillion prisms in this machine and they made up an infinite number of tiny reflections . . ."

I understood the meaning of his words as they filtered through the light in my mind. I could even see the machine he spoke of. It was a great crystal ball throwing off an uncountable number of rainbow-colored beams of light.

". . . this machine was one-of-a-kind," John continued, "built by our ancestors who were very wise and very patient. It is believed among my people that the ancients placed all of their knowledge into the crystal globe so that in times of great stress we could come to them and ask for advice."

"An' so that big glass ball got the answer to anything you wanna know?" I asked.

"In a way," John said.

We were standing in an open field of grass surrounded by a dozen or more live oaks. The sun was high but the air was almost cool. And even though I was scared of going into battle against Wall I was also deeply happy to be learning things that no other human being had ever known.

"You see," John said, "it is the custom among my people that every citizen gets to ask only one question of the Queziastril —"

"The what?"

"Queziastril was the name of our glass machine."

"Was?"

"The Calash attacked us and destroyed Queziastril so as to keep it from revealing their plan to rip the fabric of existence."

"But you knew anyway," I said.

"Yes. But knowledge is a strange thing," John replied. "A thousand people might ask Queziastril the same question and for each person the machine would give a different answer."

"Maybe yo machine was broken," I speculated.

John grinned.

"No," he said. "What would the answer be if I asked you how long it would take you to run around this field of grass?"

"I dunno," I said. "With the speed you give me I expect it would be pretty quick."

"Now what if I asked Flore the same question?"

"Big Mama don't run," I said. "She on'y walk, an' not too fast neither."

"So the answers would be different."

"I see what you mean," I said. "For everyone ask yo machine how to do sumpin' there would be a different way."

"And so," John said, "when I went to Queziastril and asked how could I stop the Calash from destroying everything . . ."

I don't know if John finished his explanation in words because suddenly it was as if I were standing in front of the great glass ball. My mind was sucked into image after image upon the reflective faces of the prisms. It was as if I were traveling down halls of pure light, one after the other.

I saw strange and alien images at the end of each hall but there was no time to ponder them because no sooner than I came to the end of one hall I was hurtled off into another. Then, finally, after seeing ten thousand fleeting scenes, I stopped before a square prism that was shiny and reflective like a silver mirror.

The image I beheld there was my own. I realized that I was seeing my own image through John's eyes many years before I was ever born. And even though I was sure that the boy I was seeing was me I seemed somehow different, not older but with much more experience. I was wondering how that could be when John started speaking again.

"You," John said, and I came out of the vision to find myself again in the grassy lea. "You were the answer Queziastril gave me. For the next five years I was granted special access and so I came back again and again to learn about you and what role you were destined to play in our war against Wall."

"And so you know everything that's going to happen?" I asked.

"No," he said. "One day the Calash came and destroyed the machine of the ancients. And also Queziastril will not allow certain information to pass through time. The machine is sentient —"

"What does that mean?" I asked.

"It is like a living thing and knows to keep certain information about the future from those living in the past. Because if you knew mistakes that you were going to make and you tried to change them the world would suffer from things that never came to pass."

"How long ago did you ask that question?" I asked John.

"Thousands of years ago."

"I wasn't even born."

"No. But time, like all other things, moves in a circle. Every moment comes back on itself. It was said that Queziastril could remember tomorrow."

That was way beyond anything I could understand at the time. Even though I contained part of Tall John's light I was still limited by the things I had known and experienced as a child and a slave on the Corinthian Plantation.

"We bettah git down to yo machine," I said then.

"Let us run," Tall John from beyond the stars said with a grin.

24.

I ran as fast as I could through the thick forest. I tried my best to keep up with John, but now he moved like the wind. Every now and then when I would lose sight of him completely I'd hear his voice in my head saying, "This way, slowpoke." And I'd follow in the direction of the thought.

After a short time I came to a ledge that looked down into a basin. John was there scanning the valley. His chest was heaving and sweat was dripping from his head and neck. Over his shoulder down about five hundred feet or so, I could see Mr. Stewart and Andrew Pike peering into a hole that resembled a freshly dug grave. Mr. Stewart was on his knees, holding up what looked like a long green stem.

"That's a part of the machine I used to come here," John said. "It once held enough power to ignite a thousand stars. But that's nothing compared to what the green powder can do."

"What now?" I said.

"We have to destroy the machine that still lies in that hole," John said.

"How big is the rest of it?" I asked.

"Like so," John said, holding his arms out as if he were holding one of Mama Flore's prize watermelons.

"Really ain't all that big," I suggested. "I guess we can fall on 'em and it'll prob'ly get broke in the jumble."

Tall John smiled. He opened his mouth as if he were about to laugh.

"No, Forty-seven," he said. "You can't just fall on my golden machine and hope it will break. That thing carried me through ten thousand suns and just as many black holes. It will take more than a clumsy boy to destroy it."

"So, what then?" I asked, a little piqued about him laughing at my ignorance.

"I will climb down the left side," John said then. "You go down to the right. When you get behind those pine trees I want you to gather up as many throwing rocks as you can. Then, when you see my signal, start throwing your rocks at Stewart and Pike. Every time after you've thrown a stone run a few steps before throwing again. You have to keep moving because Stewart will be shooting at you."

"Shootin' what?" I asked. "He don't have no gun."

"You don't want to find out, brother."

Brother. It was a word that I had heard most of my life. There was Brother Bob who called us all his brothers, and there were the slaves that had the same mother, there were the male puppies from the same litter, but never had the word meant so much to me. John, after only a few days, had become my brother. He was as close to me as my hands or feet. His pain would be my pain and his people were my own. This kinship, this relation, was even more important to me than my newly found freedom. Because the love in our hearts for each other, even though an expanse as large as the Universe divided us, was the power that would save both his race and mine.

I didn't have long to consider these thoughts though. I ran down into the woods and gathered a dozen stones.

I squatted down behind an old pecan tree. Most of the branches were dead, and only one still bore fruit. I stared across the field to where Mr. Stewart and Andrew Pike were working with a rope and pulley, trying to pull something heavy out from the grave.

Up at the top of the gorge I saw John stand and hold up a hand. A flash appeared. Pike noticed the light somehow and turned away from the winch.

"Keep digging!" Pike shouted at his ghoul. Then he strode off up the hillside toward the place where the flash had originated. I could see that my friend was hidden again.

As soon as he was a dozen steps from the excavation I hurled my first stone at Stewart. My aim was true and the rock clocked the ex-slave-boss on the forehead.

He felt the blow but didn't go down like I expected him to. Instead he gazed in my direction for three seconds, maybe four. In that short span his metal eye-patch began to glow, and then a crackling flash of light burst forward in my direction.

The tree I stood under exploded into flames, and then I remembered that John told me to keep on moving. I ran twenty steps, stopped, and threw another stone. The rock hit Stewart but at the same time his eye flared and the earth blew up under my feet.

From the ground I could see that Pike had turned around. When he laid eyes on me he began to run back down the hill.

"Go back to the hole!" he yelled at Stewart.

But Stewart didn't hear because he was cursing my number and running right at me.

At the same time John came out from hiding and was running toward the hole. Pike turned to pursue but John was moving faster. I hefted my largest rock and crouched down.

Then the most amazing thing happened. Pike's body fell away like a shirt that someone had thrown off while running. From the cloth of skin a full-grown, winged Calash flapped its great blue wings, speeding toward the hole. Now he and Tall John were moving near the same speed at their destination.

I couldn't worry about them right then because Stewart was only five steps from me. I hurled the stone with all my might, hitting him on the metal eye-patch. There was a great blue spark that jumped off the torturer's metal eye. He flipped in the air and hit the ground with a loud *humph!*

I threw another stone at the Calash named Wall but missed.

chapter twenty-four

He and John dove into the hole at the same time, it seemed.

I ran toward them with a rock in each hand.

Just when I reached the hole, Wall flew out with a golden ball clutched within his tentacles. I threw both rocks but they just bounced off of his pale hide.

The great black eye turned toward me. In the brief instant that Wall looked at me he seemed to know everything about me. He knew the history that my blood held. He knew every thought and fear I'd ever known.

I knew that he was laughing, laughing at my weakness and ignorance and fear.

And even though the only thing I wanted to do was run away I yelled and leaped forward. I didn't care if I broke every bone in my body, I would still stop Wall from stealing my brother's Sun Ship.

A voice in my head said, "Good-bye, Forty-seven. What I do now will give you the time to prepare for Wall's final attack. And remember, if you think of me I will be there."

Wall must have heard the voice in my head because he screamed then and flew high in the air. He was trying, it seemed, to free his tentacles from the golden ball . . .

. . . and then they both exploded in the air like a thousand sticks of dynamite.

I was thrown to the ground, and for a long time there was nothing but darkness.

25.

When I came to I was on my back, looking up at the sky. I got up on one shoulder to see if Mr. Stewart was still where he had fallen. He was gone but a little way beyond I saw the prone body of my brother in light — Tall John from beyond Africa.

I tried to make it to my feet but I was too groggy from the explosion. After trying to get up and falling five or six times I settled on crawling to my friend's side.

He was in a bad way. Both his arms and both of his legs were broken. There were a dozen cuts on his face and one deep gash in his chest.

His glassy eyes stared up at nothing. I was sure that he was dead, but I couldn't believe it.

"Where's yo yellah bag, John?" were the first words I said.

Then I put my face on the ground, suddenly made even weaker at the loss of my friend.

"There's no healing this body again, Forty-seven," he said.

I looked up to see him turn slightly in order that he might see me.

"John!" I shouted. "You're alive!"

"Would you please hold up a hand to block the sun from my eyes," he said weakly, and then added, "my friend."

I held my hand to shield his eyes and asked, "What can I do, John?"

"Listen," he said. "I am going to the Upper Level now."

"Where that?"

"It is the river of dreams where we all flow together."

"Like heaven?"

John nodded and coughed and then he said, "I will come to you many times over your life, Forty-seven. I'll come and help you when I can . . . with your fight against Wall."

"Ain't he dead?" I asked, feeling a prickling along my spine as if the evil one-eyed monster were staring at me at that moment.

"No," John said. "He survived the explosion but he's very weak and will not appear to you again for seventeen years at least. But when you see his evil plans imprinted on the world you must stand against him, even though you will feel small and weak compared to his power."

"How do you know what he'll do if you dyin'?" I asked, even though the question hurt my heart.

"I will come to you," he whispered. "You will be a great hero and I will be the hero's friend."

"You gonna be a ghost?" I asked, fearful of being haunted but even sadder over the loss of my friend.

"No," he hissed. "Do you remember the crystal machine that I told you about?"

"Queziastril," I said, remembering the word through the light in my mind.

"Through her I have spoken to you many times."

"I don't remember those talks, John."

"That's because you haven't had them yet . . . ," he said, and then he took a deep and painful breath. He coughed and moved his head and neck like he was going to get up but instead he fell back, and I knew that Tall John was dead.

When I could stand I dragged John's body down to the pit where Wall and his ghoul had dug up the Sun Ship. I lowered my friend into the grave and used the spade Stewart had used to cover him.

My right foot hurt me some. I guess I must have sprained it running away from Stewart's blasts. So I used the green stem as a walking stick and made my way back toward my friends.

Near the ledge, where we first spied Stewart and Pike, I found John's yellow sack.

Because of my limp the trek took me many hours.

That was the saddest journey of my young life. I was free but my friend was dead. And his passing left a void in my heart where I never knew I had something to lose. At times along the way I'd fall down on my knees and yowl some incomprehensible words to try and express the loss of my pal — Tall John from beyond Africa.

* * *

I reached the flat rock at just about sunset.

I was sad about the death of John and Mud Albert, about the slaves running in the wilderness and being hunted down by dogs. I even felt sorry for poor Eloise and the death of her father, my one-time master. But the hardest thing would be to tell Eighty-four, Tweenie, that the man she loved was dead.

She cried and caterwauled like a deep forest creature, and her grief called mine forward and I fell to the ground and wept bitterly with her. My friend was dead. He died, I knew, saving all the peoples of Earth.

When night came we moved north into a wood that I knew was uninhabited.

I could tell that the wood was safe because when I gazed hard at the valley of pines a soft gray light washed the images in my mind. I knew somehow that the gift of light that John had given me was telling me that no one would molest us in that pleasant vale.

There we found a cave that we used as a shelter. We stayed for a fortnight, until we were all healed and rested.

There was a rill not far from the mouth of our shelter. In the early morning and late at night Champ and I would steal down there and catch fish with a net I found in John's yellow bag. We had to eat the fish raw because none of us knew if John's little disk machine would keep the slave hunters from smelling smoke.

*   *   *

One afternoon I stole away from the cave and climbed way up into a willow tree. There I sat and thought about my friend.

"Hello, boy," a small, squeaky voice called.

Hearing those words I was so startled that I almost lost my balance and fell from the branch where I was sitting.

"Who?" I said, looking all around.

"Up here," the little voice said.

I looked up and there, standing on nothing but air, was a tiny little person who had orange and purple skin and a fire, like a candle's flame, hovering above his head.

"John!" I cried. "It's you!"

"I'm sorry," the true form of my friend said, "but you are mistaking me for someone else. My name is N'clect. Have you met someone else of my race?"

"No," I said. "You are looking into the future through Queziastril. You sail across the universe using suns as your propellers to come and find me."

"How do you know about Queziastril?" Little John asked. "It is the most closely guarded secret of my people."

"I know you think so," I said. "But someday soon the Calash are going to break into your hive an' break that crystal ball to pieces."

"You know about the Calash and the Talam?" Little John was amazed.

I was surprising him as much as he did me when we first

met (was that only a week before?) on the path between the slave graveyard and the slaves' quarters.

"I know a lot about you, Neglect," I said, mispronouncing his Talamish name. "You are my best friend and my brother. You came to Earth to find me and to tell me that I, Forty-seven, will fight a war against a creature of the Calash called Wall."

"Wall is their greatest warrior," John said. "Surely you must be what you say. Tell me more of the future, my friend."

And so I began the long story of the past week or so that I had shared with the little being who didn't remember any of it because for him none of it had happened yet. It started much as this book did. I had to explain the concept of slavery very carefully because he had never heard of such a thing. When I told him that white people owned everything, even the ground and the trees, and saw all other colors of people as inferior, he was doubly amazed.

"But that seems so silly," N'clect, who was destined to become Tall John, said.

We talked for hours. Sometimes I would say things that he didn't seem to hear. For instance, when I tried to explain why we were thrown into the Tomb the words came out all garbled so neither one of us understood. After I tried to explain two or three times John seemed to think that he knew why the words got confused.

"Queziastril must be interfering with the transmission," he said. "Tell me something else."

He became very somber when I told him about his death. I was about to explain the particulars on how he died when he interrupted me.

"I don't think I want to know how I die," he said. "It might sadden me too much."

I understood how he felt and resolved never again to tell the story of Tall John's death. I have been true to that resolution until writing this story.

"You must never tell anyone on your planet about these amazing experiences or about your mission," John said to me at one point in our talk.

"Why?" I asked. "Maybe somebody like Champ could help me."

"If people were to learn about your powers before they're ready, they might hurt themselves or you in the attempt to steal them."

I promised that I wouldn't tell, but that reminded me of something else.

"There's a lot I don't understand myself," I said to the floating elf.

"What?"

"I have this yellah bag," I said, holding up John's treasure.

"Oh that's grand!" the tiny elf shouted. "All you have to do is reach in and close your hand and you will, most likely, grab onto something that will help you in your mission. And over the days that come if you keep the object in your hand or pocket it will speak through the light I gave you, and you will come to know how to use it."

We talked through the night. Me sitting on that high branch and John standing on air thousands of years before and a universe away.

Toward dawn I asked, "You know, John, sometimes all you have to do is walk from the house out to the fields and you find people who speak the same tongue as you but they talk so different that you can't hardly understand a word they say."

"Yes," he said.

"So how do I know what you're saying when you're so far away an' you haven't even heard about me yet?"

"Queziastril," John said simply, and I understood everything.

The crystal translated our thoughts and so we understood each other.

When the sun peaked over the mountains John began to fade.

"Don't go!" I cried.

"Queziastril is turning to some other concern, my friend, Forty-seven. But don't fear, I'll come back and look for you again."

With those words my little friend faded into the air. And even though I was sad at his death I knew that we would be comrades for many years to come.

Something I have learned over the years since those times is that nothing is ever truly gone from the world. No atom or electron ceases to exist, they only change from one thing into another. And no life ever ends but itself transmutes into other forms and places.

John was alive in my heart and so I was able to glean a lesson that he meant to teach me.

And what I needed to do was to consider his words and make sure that I and my friends could survive long enough to do battle with Wall and his ghoul, Mr. Stewart.

Every day we saw white men in the distance searching with hounds and muskets.

One evening Champ came running into our cave, dragging Bitter Lee, slave Number Seventeen from the Corinthian Plantation. Lee had been shot in the back but still he managed to throw off the hounds and escape. Champ had found him near the stream, barely conscious and burning with fever.

"Why'd they shoot you, Bitter Lee?" Mama Flore asked him.

"They blames the slaves fo' burnin' down Corinthian," he said. "They say it was niggers killed all them white men and women."

"But didn't nobody tell'em 'bout Mr. Stewart and his band'a thieves?" Champ asked.

"None'a the white peoples from Corinthian lived," Bitter Lee said. "They's all dead 'cept for Miss Eloise, who showed up outta nowhere. She said that you niggers gone west but she didn't remember the fire or the attack."

Somehow I knew that Tall John had helped Eloise to forget the events of that terrible night. Maybe if he knew that the slaves would have been blamed for the murders he would have done differently.

"How you know all this?" Nola asked, "if you been runnin'?"

"They caught me," Number Seventeen said. "Caught me and told me that they was gonna hang me for all them murders. They th'owed me in chains but in the night Miss Eloise come to me an' unlocked my chains. She said that she had a dream that Forty-seven here had saved her, and in the dream he told her that there was no nigger or master and she thought that that meant she should let me free."

We all looked at each other, wondering what spell John had put on Eloise to make her act like that. And while we were looking at each other Bitter Lee began coughing. It was a deep, wet, rolling cough that went on for well over a minute. And when he stopped coughing he was dead.

We buried Bitter Lee at midnight. When Mama Flore was saying a few holy words over his shallow grave we heard dogs braying and even saw lantern light not twenty-five feet from where we were praying.

Later on I picked up the little disk that we used to hide us from the search parties. Physical contact with the device gave me information about its use. Somehow, the light that John gave me allowed me to understand his technology in this way. I saw that the machine's power was running low, and soon the white men would find us. So I reached into John's yellow sack and came out with a small glass plate that had blue and red threads running through it.

I studied that plate for three days without eating or sleeping.

Mama Flore and Champ and Nola and even sad Tweenie tried to get me to rest and sup but I told them that this was the only way for me to save their lives. I told them that but for all my fasting and staring in three days I hadn't learned a thing about the little glass dish.

But then, at the end of the third day, when I was feeling dizzy and weak, something strange happened.

It was as if the world stopped but I kept on going. I rose up out of my body and looked at the plate held by my body's hands. The blue and red threads wound together and waved toward one side of the rim. When I looked toward that rim I saw mountains and deep forests with trees older than countries and bears that stood twice as tall as tall men stand.

Canada. The word sounded in my mind. *Freedom.* This word rung true.

I snapped out of the trance and said out loud, "Follow the blue and red threads and they will lead us to freedom in Canada."

When the morning broke I told my friends that we were going to take a journey through the wild woods of America and go all the way to Canada, where they might let a colored man or woman be free.

"How do you know what way's the right way?" Champ Noland asked.

"Because," Tweenie said, "he an' John shared the light and now Forty-seven is the one to lead us."

There were tears in her eyes and a deep sadness in her voice. Everyone listening believed her, even me. And so that night we set out through the woods. We had over fifteen hundred miles to travel on bare feet. There were wild animals and evil white men we passed along the way. We had many adventures and each of us nearly died more than once. But we made it to Canada and freedom. Mama Flore was able to settle down on a farm that Champ started. He married Tweenie and they adopted Nola and me. And for some time we all lived together safe from chains and whips.

Maybe some other time I will tell the story of our escape or of the times years later when I came up against Mr. Stewart and other ghouls of the evil Calash — Wall.

But for the time being this story is over. Some of us lived, others did not. But at least for some of us there was happiness and freedom at the end of the trail.